AF442510

Alma and the Nuns

Alma and the Nuns

By

Sylvia Tromsö

This is a work of fiction. Similarities to real people, places, or events are entirely coincidental.
Alma and the Nuns
Copyright © 2021 Sylvia Tromsö.
ISBN: 9798771570723

1

Cleanliness
is next to Godliness

Alma and her friends all walked upright and in an orderly fashion into the changing room, all wearing only their underwear; a light cotton top and some simple, unadorned panties. Sister Sara slid silently in after them, it was her job to see to it that they all cleaned up properly, like good decent girls, and that none of them did anything indecent while they showered. Like what could they do in the showers? Alma wondered. They were only girls there, and they just woke up, they weren't in the mood for anything indecent.

There were 32 of them, and the showers only had space for 10 at a time, so they had to go in batches, but Sister Sara made them all undress at the same time anyway. They were used to getting undressed in front of Sister Sara. Sister

Maria and Sister Francesca weren't as obtrusive, their nun-habits worked like invisibility cloaks for them.

Getting undressed in front of the nuns had been weird at first, but Sister Sara had been unobtrusive back then, she had just stood quietly by and watched them slip out of their undies. But Alma still had not liked having her there, and she still didn't. That woman, Sara, was the youngest of the nuns, only 25, but to Alma and her friends that was ancient as the pyramids. She was a thin, stately woman with an easy smile and large, friendly eyes on her firm and strong but feminine face. Alma believed her to be myopic, by the way she squinted at her, but it didn't appear to inhibit her. Sister Sandra was an assistant to the Mother Superior, and stood out from all the other nuns in her attire, wearing a black dress with shoulder straps instead of the long nun-frock.

Sister Sara stood back and let the dozen girls undress and put away their undies, which Sister Maria would then remove and replace with clean ones. Sister Maria was approaching middle age, quiet, and always felt invisible to Alma and the other girls. Sister Fransesca was the same, always friendly and quiet. Sister Fransesca wasn't used to be dragged into the changing room by Sister Sara, and she blushed and looked away from the nude girls. Alma gave Sister Sara a look as she put her undies in the pile. Sister Sara silently watched over them. Alma was sure that she detected longing in her eyes, and felt a little self-conscious and blushed a little, standing nude before her.

The first batch of girls filed into the shower, Alma was one of them, one of nine, and Sister Sara stood by the doorway into the shower room and watched them bathe. The girls who's turn would be next to get in the showers stood naked beside and behind Sister Sara and would peer inside the showers, to see how long they might wait. Alma often wondered if Sister Sara didn't feel a little bit silly being the only clothed person in the changing room, especially as she saw her standing there in the doorway, with those nude girls standing all around her, looking into the showers with her. Sister Sara told them to be sure to clean all their areas well, especially their crotch. Alma thought Sister Sara showed too much interest in their crotch hygiene. She had mentioned it to her friend Tinna, who agreed. Tinna was Alma's age, the same height and shape, with long wavy black hair. That was how people told them apart, Alma had the wavy brown hair, Tinna had the wavy black hair. Not that they were that similar, not more similar than any of the other girls, apart from their hairstyles.

Alma made sure to wash her pubes and her slit very well. It could be very uncomfortable for any of them who didn't, so she made sure. She washed with soap, lathering well, and she rubbed, and she rinced herself off, and then she ran her finger through her slit and smelled it. She nodded to herself, she had done a good job.

One of the new girls, Tove, an unremarkable blonde haired tomboy with shoulder-length hair and slight curves looked at Alma, making a face. It was an expression of discomfort. Alma gave Tove a serious look, and motioned for her to wash better. Tove shook her head, red faced. Alma's shoulders sagged when she saw that Tove was ignoring her.

"She's going to love her first day here," said Tinna, who had been watching the exchange of hand-signals between them.

"We should have told her when she arrived here yesterday."

"Maybe someone told her, maybe she just didn't listen."

"Maybe she didn't believe."

"She'll believe all sorts of things when she gets out."

They turned off the showers and filed out. The next batch of nine girls walked in, breasts jiggling. This batch had two new girls, and Alma and Tinna felt sorry for them. They had only six towels with which to dry themselves, and Alma and Tinna counted themselves lucky to be among the first girls to get use of the towels. Sometimes they were in the third batch, and then they got to dry themselves with wet towels. Then it could get cold standing there in the nude, waiting for Sister Sara to inspect them.

While the last five girls were showering, Sister Sara had them all line up, side by side for their inspection. They had to form three lines to fit in the room, one after another. Sister Maria had arrived there to help Sister Sara, and stood by noncommittally, just waiting to come in and help if there was an issue. Sister Fransesca stood at the other end of the lines, waiting, not sure what her function was. Alma and Tinna looked out at the new girls to catch a glimpse of them before the inspection began, to see how they were taking it yet. They had all just lined up when the last batch of five girls came out of the shower, and Sister Maria handed them the towels that she had just wrung.

Tove looked uncomfortable, she was standing in line holding one hand over her slit and one over her nipples.

"Hands down by your sides," said Sister Sara. She glared at Tove, who looked more uncomfortable. Sister Sara walked to her, situated herself facing her, and said in a gentle voice: "put your hands down. What are you hiding girl? Don't feel ashamed, we're all girls here."

Tove slowly uncovered herself, and made to stand upright in front of Sister Sandra with her arms by her sides. He cheeks were pink with embarrassment.

"Now part your feet, like so, one foot apart," said Sister Sara in a gentle tone, and helped spacing Tove's feet by putting her own foot between her legs, and Tove widened her stance, red faced. Sister Sara smiled at her, then stepped back to see them all together.

"Look at you, all looking so clean and dry. So young, so beautiful," she said, beholding the young, slick bodies in front of her, all presented without a stitch as nature intended.

Alma always got the creeps at Sister Sara's little pre-inspection speech. She saw Sister Maria stood by the end of the line, holding a towel.

"You know girls, that cleanliness is next to Godliness," said Sister Sara as she walked between the last line of girls and the middle line, examining them as she went. She looked at the three new girls from behind, "we don't use perfume to disguise or hide our body odor here."
She walked to the end of the line of the beautiful nude bodies, still talking, turned around and walked along between the middle line and the first line, glancing at the new girls. She came to the end: "turn around please, slowly," she told Maria, the pudgy one. Maria turned around,

while sister Sara ran her eyes over her bare skin, front and back. "Good, no tattoos. A body unadorned with ink is a modest body." She repeated the formula with the other two new girls, before walking to the end of the line.

"Arms up," she told the first girl in the front line, who complied, and Sister Sara ran her hands down her arm and through her armpit-fur, and then she leaned in holding the girl by the waist and smelled her armpits while the girl put her hands on the top of her head, and Sara smiled with approval and she looked down on the girl's furry slit. Shaving the pubes was not the style in the school, the nuns considered it immodest, so that all of the girls had a very nice and soft tuft of hair down there, and Sister Sara smiled as she stroked it gently, having it waft across her palm, and then very gently ran her finger through the girl's slit, between her labia. The girl shook a little, they always did when Sister Sara did this to them. Sister Sara brought her finger up to her face and smelled it, nodded with approval, smiled at the girl, Sister Maria handed her the towel to dry her finger on, and she moved to the next girl.

Sister Sara repeated the process to the next girl. It was the same process, every morning: they showered, lined up, Sister Sara smelled them and fingered their pussy. Alma had heard rumors that most of the girls went to their rooms afterwards and masturbated until orgasm, or else they would feel unfulfilled for the whole day. Alma knew that she wanted to do that, so she believed the rumors. The only difference was when they had their periods. Then Sister Sara left them alone.

There were four girls in line before Alma's turn came, giving her time to prepare mentally, although she was getting used to this. Sister Sara didn't need to tell Alma to raise her hands, she did it when her turn came, and Alma didn't look her in the eye when Sister Sara ran her hands over her body. Alma closed her eyes when Sara leaned in and smelled her armpits, and kept them closed while she ran her fingers through her tuft of pussy-hair. She took a deep breath and relaxed, hands on the top of her head. Sister Sara had a very gentle touch, Alma had to admit that, and her soft, loving strokes across her labia in preparation for the more invasive test were actually pretty pleasant. Then Sara's finger slid inside Alma's slit, slowly sliding from back to front, Sara gently forced her fingers deep inside, pleasantly stimulating Alma's clit, and Alma couldn't help but to shake, none of the girls could, and she got moist. But Sister Sara didn't stop fingering her, but ran her finger back between her labia once more, now slick with Alma's femine juices, and Alma felt her rub her slit gently, bringing her closer to God. Alma's eyes cracked open, and she saw Sister Sara's gentle expression as she felt around and then slowly entered her finger inside Alma's slida. This was also something that she did from time to time. She said she was checking the girl's hymen. That was a thing of great importance to the nuns. Three or four girls were subjected to a hymen check every morning like this, and there was hell to pay if it was in any way damaged.

Sister Sara slid her wet fingers out of Alma's slida as she was on the verge of orgasm, and brought them up to her nose. She licked her finger, looking Alma in the eyes. Alma secretly wished to go to her room and masturbate, to finish the work that Sara had begun, but she never could. Tinna always followed her and talked with her. Alma didn't want to masturbate with Tinna. She watched Sister Sara wipe her fingers on the towel and move to Tinna. Tinna raised her hands as Alma lowered hers, and Alma took a few deep breaths as she watched Sister Sara stimulate her, only to leave her unfulfilled.

Sister Sara arrived at Tove, and she told Tove to lift her arms above her head, which Tove reluctantly did. Sister Sara approved of Tove's armpits, and she slid her fingers though her slit while Tove, red in the face, bit her lips and closed her eyes, looking very uncomfortable about this, and Sara brought her Tove-juice covered finger to her nose and had a whiff. And she frowned and she said angrily: "you haven't cleaned properly. Step back and get out of line."

Tove looked up at Sister Sara with a worried look in her eyes. Sister Sara pushed her back a step, then moved to the next girl, followed by Sister Maria. Tove walked between the lines of girls and Sister Fransesca directed her to stand by the shower opening.

The next girl yelped like a puppy when Sister Sara gently, but firmly and ever so slowly checked for her hymen. It took almost a minute, her soft moans echoing in the changing room. None of the girls dared look her way.

Sister Sara found another girl with a dirty vagina and had Sister Fransesca lead her to the showers to stand beside Tove before she came to the second new girl, who also turned out to have neglected her vaginal hygiene, and had to step back and join Tove and that other girl. The third new girl had also not cleaned herself well enough, and joined the group.

"Your vaginas are good enough to eat off," Sister Sara told the girls still standing in line, licking her lips, regarding them with approval. The girls were still with their hands on the top of their head. She continued, "and you should be proud of yourselves, at being so cleanly. You can get dressed now. Not the four of you!" she said in a harsh tone to the four girls that she had found to be less hygienic: "you need to go and shower again, and clean yourselves this time." The girls looked sheepishly at Sister Sara, and at each other. "Wait!" called Sister Sara, and she turned around, and walked to Alma, who was standing around waiting for Sister Maria to hand her some undies. "Alma, come here," said Sister Sara, tugging Alma with her by her arm, and she introduced her to the four girls: "you are always so clean, you can teach them to clean their vagina."

 Alma felt more uncomfortable than she'd ever felt before, but Sister Sara wasn't a person to be argued with, and she ordered them into the shower room again, and she stood in the doorway and watched them.

 Alma gave it her best, and she showed the new girls and that one girl who just hadn't been feeling it this morning how to lather the soap before applying it, and then rubbing the foam into every crevise of the vagina.

 "Then you put your fingers in your slit and smell it," she told them her secret, showed them. They watched her, red-faced, and one by one, did as she showed them. Tove smelled her finger, an decided to wash again. When they were ready, their pussies as clean as they could be, they went out of the shower room again, and Sister Sara stepped out of their way and handed them each a towel.

Most of the other girls were fully dressed when they came out of the shower. Sister Maria was handing them their school-uniforms, their plaid skirt and light cotton blouse that they wore over their undies. Alma and the new girls watched while they dried themselves as all the rest of the girls got their school dress on. It was humiliating.

Alma remembered her first days, when she had had to shower twice. That wasn't long ago, just last year, and she remembered how uneasy she had felt at undressing with all those other girls for the first time. She'd never been naked with strangers before back then, but it had turned out okay, since the other girls had been undressing too, but she had never met any of them until just the day before and they hadn't had any time to talk or get to know each other. And then the were all naked, and it felt awkward and uneasy going to the showers with them. She'd been in the second batch then, and she'd felt the anticipation while watching the first batch shower before her. It had felt funny, standing beside the fullu clothed Sister Sara in the nude and watching the girls shower. Sister Sara had felt a little bit like an alien to her; the only one fully dressed. And when her turn came, she had felt too awkward and embarrassed to wash her vagina with the other girls, even though they made signs for her to do so. Like Tove now, she hadn't heeded their warnings, it had looked too much like masturbation to her, and she'd not felt right doing it, and come out of the shower and the other girls had given her worried looks while they all waited for the rest of the girls to join them. Alma had not been at all that bothered by having Sister Sara slide her fingers through her slit, but she still remembered her disapproving look as she smelled her finger afterwards, and she could remember every minute of her shower alone in that large cavernous room, watched by Sister Sara. She had told her what do to, stood over her while she did. And then she come back from the shower, completely bare-assed naked, and found all the other girls had gotten dressed and were waiting for her. She could feel their eyes on her naked body as she dried herself, and then Sister Maria, although that had been a different Sister Maria; there where three Sister

Marias in the school, had taken her towel, and she had stood there, all exposed while all those fully clothed girls stood around and watched. Sister Maria had told them why Alma had been in the shower again, and she even held Alma's hands behind her back so she wouldn't cover herself while she paraded her along the line, humiliating her. The girls had all been extra nice to her for the following week. The first day it had only been her, then on the second day she got to share her humiliation with Tinna. They both felt a little better not being the only one naked. They had been friends since.

All the girls knew how Tove and Maria and Pippa felt. And Hanna should have known better. Sister Sara stood, her arms folded, and watched them all. She walked up to Alma when Sister Maria had taken her towel and said to her: "now you must inspect them."

 Alma's eyes grew wide. "Me? I can't!"

"Sure you can, you know how body odor smells? You just smell them, and if they have body odor, they must wash again. Then you have to put your finger inside their vagina and smell it, and if they don't smell, they get to put their clothes on. Come, I'll guide you."

The four girls lined up, and put their hands up on top of their head. They eyed the other girls, who were already clothed, and stood by just quietly watching them, not mockingly but empathetically, as they had all experienced this. Maria was first in line, then Tove. Tove looked so thin and shapely next to Maria, but Maria, although she was pudgy, had very firm and shapely boobs, not sagging at all. Alma stood herself in front of Maria, and smiled awkwardly at her, "sorry," she told her, and she held her right shoulder while she smelled her left armpit, and then vice versa. She looked at Sister Sara when she had done this, and she smiled and waited. Alma looked at Maria, and tried to smile. She felt grossly uncomfortable, but she moved her hand sofly across Maria's soft and ample side, then between her thighs, and up until she felt her pubes. "Could you...?" she asked Maria, who didn't react immediately, until Alma looked down and wiggled her hand in between her thighs. Maria moved her feet apart. Alma nodded and gave her a friendly smile. She paused, Maria closed her eyes, and so did Alma as she slowly reached up to touch Maria's slit.

"You have to go in," Sister Sara reminded her in a soft tone of voice.

Alma pressed her finger in between Maria's labia, feeling her moist interior. She had never put her finger inside another girl's pussy before, and felt embarrassed, doubly so because she could feel the eyes of all her friends upon her own naked body as she did it. It was probably best that they were both naked, or this would have felt more of a violation to Maria. She could feel Maria's inner labia as she slid her finger slowly along her clit. Maria gasped.

"Now smell her," said Sister Sara.

Alma came out of her reverie, and she pulled her finger out of Maria's slit, and brought it to her nose and smelled it. It smelled clean. Sister Sara confirmed, smelling Maria's pussy-juice on Alma's finger. Sister Maria wiped Alma's finger with a towel, and Alma moved on over to Tove.

"I'm so sorry," she whispered to Tove as she smelled her armpits, "but we tried to warn you." And she took a deep breath before she ran her hand between Tove's thighs, and as gently as she could she ran her finger through her slit.

Alma did her work slowly and diligently, trying her best to be gentle with the girls. She turned around and found all the other girls standing there quietly around them, watching them sympathetically. She stood by and watched the new girls get dressed, and gave them all a little hug to make them feel better, saying: "now you're one of us," before she started getting dressed.

All the pretty clean maidens filed out of the room, smelling like sunshine.

2

Sister Sara's offer

Once they had exited the dressing room, Sister Sara pointed Alma to come with her. Alma felt uncomfortable, following Sister Sara to her little offices. It was a sparse room, undecorated, with just a simple wooden desk and two chairs, and shelves with the school records dating back 20 years. A window overlooked the school grounds.

"Have a seat," said Sister Sara, pointing Alma to sit in front of her. Alma sat down, and Sister Sara took her seat opposite her. Sara leaned forward and tented her fingers and began: "you did well. It was your first time inspecting the girls, and you did it like a pro."

Alma sat straight in her chair, hands on her lap, not moving a muscle.

"You can relax, I'm not going to punish you. Actually I have an offer to make you."

Alma nodded slowly.

"I want you to do the inspections in case I have to go away, for whatever reason. Do you think you can do that?"

Alma swallowed hard, she was not liking where this was going, but she nodded anyway and she replied: "great!"

"Also, I need some help with the physical checkups that will be coming up. I've already spoken to the older girls, and they've done it before and are alright with helping out. Not all of the nuns feel that it is proper for them, as it involves seeing the boys without their clothes on."

"I have to see the boys... naked?"

"Yes. It's the physical exam, we measure them. Just like you and the girls, you remember?"

Alma nodded, she remembered. They had all been naked, and the nuns had measured them. She hadn't remembered any boys being there though. But that offer actually sounded not too bad. She would like to see that boy, Gunnar, that she liked. She wondered if she could be alone with him, when he was naked?

"Good, I knew I could count on you," said Sister Sara.

Sister Sara stood up, and Alma did the same, and they shook hands. Sister Sara showed Alma out the door, and Alma went back to her dorm to see Tinna, and tell her about Sister Sara's offer.

"So you have to masturbate us girls, but you will get to see the boys naked?" said Tinna.

"Yes. That's the deal."

"Can I join you? We could split up our work, you masturbate us, I get to see the boys naked?"

"No, I can't do that."

"You could ask her."

***

The next morning Sister Sara made Alma do a practice examination. Sister Sara knocked on her room, and woke both her and Tinna an hour early: "it's time, you need to get cleaned up," said Sister Sara.

"Can I go too?" asked Tinna, half asleep.

"No. You stay here."

Alma got dressed and followed Sister Sara through the hallways, and up the stairs.

"Where are you taking me?"

"You're going to take a bath," Sister Sara said in

an easy tone.

"A bath?"

"Yes, you need to be properly cleaned up when you do my job. It would be terribly humiliating to be expected to send girls with smelly vaginas to the shower while having a smelly vagina yourself."

"Oh..." Alma nodded in understanding. They walked further. "I was wondering, can Tinna help me when we go do the physical examination?"

Sister Sara looked Alma in the eye and made a slight grin as she said:

"She wants to see the boys naked?"

Alma felt her face grow red.

Sister Sara smiled: "of course she can, if you feel that you need her help. Can you trust her?"

"Of course I can, she's my best friend."

They came to a door, and Sister Sara opened it and showed Alma in: "this is my chambers."

It was a small room, with just a small desk by the wall, a bed, with a bedstand with the bible on top of it, and a bath-tub in the corner. The tub was already full, and steamy.

"That's my bath-tub, this is where I get cleaned.

And you get to stay here when I need you to take over, in case I need you to do that, that is. Please, be my guest."

Alma looked at Sister Sara.

"I'll wait here."

Alma wrinkled her forehead.

"Go ahead. Take off your clothes. Don't mind me, we're all girls here."

Alma slowly began unbuttoning her blouse.

"You'll be here all day. Come on, I've seen you before."

"I had my friends with me then."

"Okay, I'll bathe with you," said Sister Sara, and slipped off her bib-skirt and began taking off her frock.

Alma sped up her undressing, watching Sister Sara as she undressed, and they got naked at the same time. Sister Sara was slim, not athletic but weak, she was small breasted and her lower ribs were visible. She had shoulder length hair under her headdress, held behind her head, and let loose it flowed around her shoulders. She had a very admirable thigh gap, and Alma was sure that the girls would all envy her of it, though the rest of her body wasn't much.

"Now step into the bath with me, don't worry if we splash water on the floor, it drains off," said Sister Sara as she gently took Alma by the arms. And Alma stepped into the bath, and lowered herself in, while Sara stood by. The bath was much more comfortable than the shower, and Alma could feel it's warm embrace pressing against her skin, so gently, so intimately. She sighed with pleasure as she lay there immersed. She wished she could relax in the tub, but now was not the time. Alma took the soap and latered herself under her arms, and Sara sat on the edge of the tub and shampooed her hair.

"Aren't you going to get in?" asked Alma.

"No, I just stripped so you would, you have to bathe by yourself, you're an adult, after all, aren't you?"

Sister Sara finished shampooing Alma's hair in the nude, then she washed the lather off in the tub, stood up, dried herself and calmly got dressed again. She sat on the edge of her bed with a cozy smile and watched Alma wash herself. Alma looked at Sister Sara as she washed, she felt more comfortable washing her vagina in the tub, for once she had that limited privacy of not having her sex ogled while she washed. She finished, and rose to her feet, letting the water drip from her. She pressed the water from her hair, and Sister Sara handed her a comb, which she used to comb out even more water, and straighten her hair. Standing there, facing Sister Sara as she sat and watched her with that calm expression on her face made Alma feel somehow more intimate with her. She felt warm and at ease and she felt that she could trust Sister Sara. Sister Sara stood up as Alma got out of the tub, and helped her dry herself.

"Let me smell you," she asked, and leaned in and smelled Alma's armpits. "You want to check yourself?"

Alma smelled her armpits, they were clean.

"Now your pussy. Come on, legs apart more, you don't need to force yourself on yourself."

Alma stood straight with half a meter space between her feet. She ran her fingers in between her labia, that she had just dried with the towel, and shook a little inside. Sister Sara nodded approvingly. Alma brought the finger to her nose and smelled. It was just regular skin odor.

"Good? I'll confirm," said Sister Sara, and she

had Alma hold her arms behind her back and she went down on her knees, and looked closely at Alma's pussy, moving her pubes with her hands, both her hands, and she leaned in and she smelled her slit from her position, with her legs doubled under her, whiffing well, and then she stuck out her tongue, and Alma could feel her explore through her pubic hairs, touching her clit, licking it, tasting it. She had her tongue inside Alma's slit, between her labia, licking her softly, gently, as Alma felt herself become moist, and Sister Sara nibbled lovingly at her inner labia, pulling it, running her tongue all over it, then moving front to her clit and sucking on it. Alma felt her juices leak down on Sara's face, and she bit her own hand as she quaked so she wouldn't let out a loud moan. Instead she moaned softly, biting her hand.

Sister Sara rose to her feet again, looked Alma in the eyes, and then she hugged her tightly, full body contact, and held Alma in her arms as if she were her lover for a good minute, stroking her back. Then she kissed Alma gently on the lips, once, twice... and Alma felt as intimate with Sara as she had ever been with anyone. If only she'd been a man...

"You're ready. Now get dressed and come with me. We have our duty to attend to."

***

The girls all showered like normal. Tinna and Tove washed extra carefully, since they knew Alma personally. Tove wasn't looking forward to it, but then, none of the girls was, really. Alma realized as she stood in the shower doorway, why Sister Sara always stood there. She was looking at the progress. It wasn't that watching ten nude girls wash themselves in the shower wasn't calming, it just beat watching some nude girls standing around waiting to shower. Alma looked back at the waiting girls, their fluffy pubes attracted her attention. She wondered if they'd look better shaved. They would be easier to clean, she knew. The tuft of hair retained sweat, which then smelled. If that were to be removed... Alma realized that she was ogling pussies. She sighed. There was nothing else but nude female bodies all around her, and she felt a little self conscious, being the only one dressed, having on her cotton blouse and pleated skirt. What if all those girls decided to push her into the shower? She'd be all wet, in her clothes, and they'd not come to any harm, being naked already. She felt anxiety over having to finger them all. She didn't need the embarrassment. Why was that even a thing? Who had decided that? She planned to not do that when Sister Sara left, leaving her in charge. But could she? Someone would tell on her. She'd be punished, somehow. Being the only one clothed was somehow worse than just being nude with the girls, being one of them, one with them, intimate, belonging. Under the warm and gentle spray of the showers, so comfortable... They didn't speak to her now that she was an outsider, marked by her concealing threads. And that's why she was reduced to looking at their bodies instead of their faces, taking them all in, instead of just making eye contact. Maybe that was how the boys saw them, long legs, thigh gap, pussy, hips, ass, flat stomach, nicely curved back, breasts... just lithe, attractive bodies.

The first batch of girls came tip-toeing out of the shower, breasts jiggling. They dried themselves, and the next batch entered, ass-cheeks jiggling. It did nothing for her sexually, but she had to admit that they were beautiful, all of them, each in their own way. Nothing is as pleasant to behold as a girl's fully sexually developed body, and thus they were at least pleasant to watch.

When the girls had lined up standing straight and placed their hands on their head, Alma went through the motions mechanically, delivering her speech in a flat monotone while she walked between the lines. It was even more surreal to walk between lines of nude girls than being a nude girl in a line. Their bodies made a pattern all lined up like that, a different on on the front than on the rear. She decided she liked their front better, it had more going on aesthetically. She was spaced out when she ran her finger through each of the girl's slit, smelled it, and determined if it was fine. One girl still smelled like pee, and she had to send her back, but the others passed. The oldest girls all grinned mischievously at Alma when they were being fingered, like they enjoyed this. Some looked betrayed. Tinna and Tove showed with their expression that they understood.

Alma felt so for that one girl that she'd sent to the shower, that when she came back from it, all clean, to a room full of fully dressed girls, she hugged her, petted her on the cheek and told her it was all right. Then she fingered her again.

3

Alma and Tinna visit the boy's changing room

The school had a boy's football team. The girl's had their own gymnastics team, but only the boys got a team sport. The girls would often sit and watch the boys rehearse their football, cheering them on. Alma liked Gunnar the best, he was the tallest, and Tinna liked Fleming and Jan, and sometimes Christian. They were all better players than Gunnar, but Alma was firmly set on Gunnar. He had such bright blue eyes, and defined facial expression and strong shoulders.

The practice game had ended, and Alma and Tinna still sat there and mused about the boys as they filed out of the field and into the school gymnasium to have a shower.

"I want to have a better look at Gunnar," said

Alma.

"What do you mean, you want to see him closer?"

"No, I want to see him naked."

"Maybe you could ask him nicely."

"I have a better idea, follow me," she said, and stood up.

"You're not gonna..."

"I am."

Alma and Tinna smiled mischievously at each other as they entered the boys changing room. The boys were still taking off their clothes after the game, and when the girls walked in on them, most of them were bare chested. One was naked: a short pudgy boy, turning his back at them as he hung up his undies, and he was startled when he turned around and saw the two girls. The girls smiled and blushed a little when they glimpsed his little limp penis flop about before he managed to cover it with his hands. They looked around in the dressing room, but Gunnar wasn't there. He had to be in the shower already. Alma headed there, and Tinna gave the embarrassed naked boy a look down, biting her lower lip before she followed after her.

He stood, with an embarrassed smile, both hands covering his peen and looked after them.

Alma and Tinna stood in the entry to the shower and looked inside. There were six boys in there, there was Ulf, Gunnar's friend, and a Jan and Lasse and his friend, and another one they didn't know the name of, and they watched them, their gleaming wet bodies under their warm streams, their limp penises swaying as they washed. The girls saw Gunnar in there, on the end, and he was the first to notice the girls. The other boys noticed them one by one, and all covered themselves, some even turning around to face the wall. Alma and Tinna smiled and blushed.

Looking Gunnar in the eye, Alma walked into the shower room, while Tinna spread her arms to cover the exit. Alma glanced at the naked boys standing in the shower as she slowly walked past them, she could see their pubes as they covered. Gunnar wasn't as bashful as they, and let his member hang in plain sight while he continued washing himself. Alma stopped in front of him, slowly looking him up, taking in his body with her eyes; his strong wide chest, his firm abs, his tick, swaying penis. It was thicker and longer than she'd been expecting, having seen Michaelangelo's statue of David. But then, all the boys had a larger peen than David. She saw that now.

"Hi," she said.

"Couldn't you have waited until I was out of the changing room?" he asked her.

"No, I wished to see you."

"Now you see me," he said, spreading his arms. "Why don't you touch me too?" He walked from under his stream, to within reach of her and shook his pelvis, so that his penis swung from one thigh to another, "go on, touch me."

Alma's blush intensified, and she took him on his words and reached out to him and got a hold on his penis.

"There," he said with a mischievous grin, "now that you have me, what will you do to me?"

Alma stood quietly as she looked down on his penis in her hand, she rubbed it, fondled it with her fingers, it was expanding, she both felt and saw, it was getting hard in her hand.

The other boys watched them, and Tinna. One of them walked up to Tinna, looking her straight in the eye, he tried to passed her, making full body contact with her. She caught him in her arm and she held him, and he held his arms around her waist, and they both stood there for a moment, just looking each other in the eyes. And she could feel it just a little too late as he started tugging her, and he caught her arm and dragged her with him into the shower room, and Jan and Lasse realized what he was doing and went to help him and they dragged Tinna under one of the showers, screaming.

Alma watched this happen, Gunnar's erection still in her hand. Two of the boys still stood there, just covering themselves with both hands and waiting for all this to be over, while two nude boys were holding Tinna under the shower fully clothed, their penises still limp and floppy. Lasse's friend walked out, but when he was just outside he stopped and looked shocked. And then Sister Sara came to view.

Sister Sara stood in the doorway to the showers and looked inside. She saw the two boys standing there on one side, covering themselves, Alma standing in the middle of the shower room just in front of Gunnar, who still had a firm erection just beside her, and on the other side was Ulf and Lasse standing with Tinna between them, and Jan, who quickly covered his peen as he saw Sister Sara.

"Girls, why are you in the boys shower?"

"We just..." said Alma.

"There are no excuses for this kind of behavior," said Sister Sara. "I know you just came here to look at their penises. You want to see an array of penises. And now you have. And now you must apologize to them, and get out of the shower."

"But..."

"No. Apologize to them. Come boys," Sister Sara looked at the two boys standing and waved them to approach her, and at Ulf and Lasse and the others. She looked at Gunnar's bouncing erecton as he walked to her, and she frowned with disapproval. She had the boys line up in the shower room, and made Tinna and Alma apologize to each of them in turn and shake their hand.

"Sorry for looking at you in the shower," they said, and shook their hand, one after another. Only those two boys still covered their penis with one hand. Gunnar still had an erection that he wasn't trying to hide. He looked proud of his erection. The girls blushed.

Sister Sara brought the girls out of the shower room, and they made to leave the dressing room, but Sister Sara held them: "where do you think you're going in those wet clothes?"

"What?" said Tinna, knowing that Sister Sara was referring to her.

"You can't go out like that, you'll catch a cold."

Tinna looked around, all the boys were still in there, as they had been when she and Alma went into the showers, and they were staring silently at her.

"You have to take them all off. One of the boys will lend you a towel. Come now."

Tinna looked at Sister Sara, suddenly afraid.

"What are you afraid of? You can't expect me to believe that you are bashful now? We're in the changing room. Take your wet clothes off."

Tinna looked uneasy, but she started taking her wet clothes off, starting with her blouse. The fabric stuck to her, and fell on the floor with a heavy, wet thud as she dropped her garments by her side. Sister Sara looked at her firmly until she had taken off her socks and panties, and she stood there naked in the middle of the boy's changing room, covering herself with her hands, looking Sister Sara in the eye. They boys were coming out of the shower, and grabbing their towels.

Sister Sara looked around: "boys, the girls will now apologize to all of you." And she had them all line up, and Alma and Tinna went between them, Tinna still in the nude, and apologized to them all and shook their hand. The pudgy boy they had first seen naked smiled at Tinna, now wearing just a towel, but this time Tinna looked ashamed. Someone lent Tinna a towel, and she wrapped herself in it before Sister Sara led the two of them out of the changing room.

4

Alma and Tinna
seek fulfillment
from each other

Sister Sara walked the girls from the boys complex to the girl's complex, and the girls who they met watched them curiously, Tinna bashfully looking away. The girls were both red faced after their activity, and Alma felt a tingle inside her and her panties were getting wet.

They had to meet the Mother Superior, who spoke to them in some firm words and had them say a few prayers before she sent them to their room without dinner as a punishment.

Locked in their room together they could analyze their adventures.

"Oh! That's how they look," said Alma, "I've only ever just seen my father's penis before."

"And now they have all seen me," said Tinna, still holding her towel in place.

"Yes, but you saw them, and that's the important thing. And you got to shower with the boys. And I touched a penis!   I touched Gunnar's penis! It was so soft, and so firm and so warm..."

"How was that? Touching him, I mean?"

"It was great. I can't wait to have it. How was showering with the boys?"

"It was wet and rough. I wasn't going to, but they pulled me in. And suddenly they weren't bashful anymore and I could see them."

"It was great, right?"

Tinna nodded.

"I'm so hot right now. I want to have sex. I want to have sex right now. Do you think we could sneak into the boys dormitories and find Gunnar and have him fuck us? I saw him, he was ready for me in the shower. He was all hard and his penis was much bigger and firmer than all the other's boys."

"And then Sister Sara will slip her finger inside you tomorrow and find your hymen breached, and she and mother superior will burn you at the stake as a whore."

Alma sighed. Then she had a thought: "but if

he sticks it in my ass? My ass doesn't have a hymen."

"I've heard you need to have a lubricant if you want to do that."

"You've heard everything. Who tells you all of these things?"

Tinna blushed.

"I'm still hot. I need to hold someone, to kiss someone at least." she looked at Tinna, "would you hold me?"

Tinna smiled, and they embraced.

"Admit it Tinna, you are also thinking about how it would be to lie under a boy and have him fuck you."

"I do."

"And you must be hot too, I mean, not only did you see all those naked boys, but you were also naked with the boys in the shower. They were naked and touching you. Their penises were flopping about between their legs while they were touching you. You were naked with naked boys. You were so close to having experienced sex, I envy you," said Alma, and she looked Tinna in the eye.

Tinna smiled.

"We both want to have sex, and we're locked in here together, two girls, so horny."

"We could pretend..."

Alma looked at Tinna: "you want to be a substitute for a boy? For me?"

"That's not what I meant."

Alma sighed, and looked Tinna in the eye, thinking. "We can't have sex, but we could lie on each other, and pretend one of us is a boy, and just close our eyes and imagine that a boy is touching us, and that we're touching a boy."

"What do you mean?"

"I mean, we get into bed and we close our eyes, and I pretend that you are a boy while I touch your body, and you pretend that I'm a boy while I touch your body, and you just imagine that a boy is touching you, and so do I."

Tinna thought about it, she nodded. "I like it, let's do it."

Alma smiled, and she started taking off her clothes. Tinna unwrapped her towel and hung it up. She was already in the buff. Once Alma had taken off her socks and stood there as nude as the day she was born, she opened her arms for Tinna, and they embraced. Nether of them felt much like she was embracing a man, since they could very clearly feel each other's breasts touching, squishing between them. They were both very soft to the touch and not muscular at all, like the boys.

"Should we kiss?" asked Tinna.

Alma thought about it. Then she nodded: "yes, definitely," and they looked at each other. Tinna blushed, and Alma felt awkward. After all, they were both girls. "Okay, let's do this," she said, and she closed her eyes and slowly moved their faces together.

"Should we lie down in bed first?" asked Tinna.

"Oh, yes, let's," said Alma, and they parted, and Alma asked: "yours or mine?"

Tinna thought: "yours," and Tinna got into Alma's bed, lay on her back and waited for Alma: "Tinna, am I supposed to be on top?"

"Oh? Don't you want to begin on top? I can get on top of you if you want?"

"No, no, this is fine, I'll get on top of you," said Alma, and she got into bed, straddling Tinna.

"This is so uncomfortable," said Tinna, looking up at Alma, who was straddling her on all fours.

"You want to quit?"

"No. I'm ready. I think I'll never get to sleep if we don't finish this."

"You're still thinking about the naked boys?"

Tinna nodded. She felt warm, she'd been naked with the naked boys. Their bare penises just a foot away from her exposed vagina. Their penises had touched her thighs in the shower. The recollection made her tingle.

"Imagine that I'm a boy," said Alma, and she lowered her body on Tinna, making full skin contact from their toes to their head, and she kissed Tinna gently on the cheek.

And as Alma lay down on Tinna she felt good, a great sense of intimacy flowed through her, and she smiled at Tinna. Their faces went passive with anticipation, their cheeks were red, their pupils were dilated, their breath was heavy. Alma thought that this is what sex would be like. But with a boy instead of Tinna, and she imagined herself lying on top of Gunnar. Actually she wanted Gunnar to lie on top of her, but she could live that fantasy later. She closed her eyes and leaned in on Tinna's face, and their lips met, so soft, so warm, and a nice warm tingle ran through Alma's whole body. They kissed more firmly, tongues touching, softly licking each other's lips, and they rolled to their side, not daring to open their eyes so as not to break their fantasy, and they started running their fingers across each others sides, sometimes grappling hands, then releasing again and continuing to touch. They could reach down to each other's ass, but they avoided touching the breasts. Alma lay on her back and let Tinna climb on top of her, lips still locked, and Tinna began pressing her thigh between Alma's legs, trying to stimulate her. She felt Alma's slit with her fingers, and spooning her, she ran her fingers in through Alma's slit like Sister Sara had done to her, and she found Alma's clit and she rubbed it between her fingers, and Alma gratefully gave Tinna a deep French kiss in return, exchanging saliva. Tinna let go of Alma's clit, and they rolled around together, kissing, exchanging more saliva, and then Alma started fondling Tinna's labia, and she invaded her slida with her fingers and rubbed her inside and outside, causing Tinna to squirm away. Alma let Tinna go and Tinna came back and they continued kissing each other's face and neck, letting their hands run wild across each other's writhing body.

Alma thought it all felt very good and cozy, and she had never felt this intimate with anyone before, but at the same time she yearned for more stimulation, she wasn't getting any release from Tinna, and every time it approached, Tinna moved her hand away, out of her. Finally, Alma got in under Tinna, and held her hand and placed it on her pussy, and whispered in her ear: "finish me. I'll finish you."

And spooning Tinna on her left side, Alma started to gently masturbate Tinna. Tinna soon got her hint, and masturbated Alma. They lay there side by side, quietly masturbating each other, as they looked up at the ceiling. Alma used her right hand, Tinna her left. And Alma smiled at their awkwardness, and Tinna smiled, and they giggled, then slowly they felt their orgasm start coming on, and Tinna started to moan, and then they each bit their other hand so as not to make a sound as they touched each other more firmly and rapidly. They each started to quake, and not knowing when to stop, they continued rubbing each other until they couldn't any more.

Fully at peace with the universe, they embraced again, and held each other, silently appreciating each other's company as they fell asleep.

5

The girls
go skinny dipping

There was a small lake a few minutes walk from the school. The girls all knew that it was there, and sometimes walked there to look at it, to walk by it and talk, and once in a while, they went swimming.

Alma and Tinna went there one day after dinner, along with some other girls their own age; Ingrid, Thalia and Tove, older girls named Liv and Anna, who were the oldest but behaved even older, and two younger girls; pudgy Maria and Samantha, who looked the most mature of them all despite being youngest.

It was very warm, the day had been bright and sunny, warming the lake, and they would have at least two hours of sunlight before they would need to return back to the dormitories. The girls were all excited when they came to the lakeshore, and the more experienced ones, Liv and Anna began taking off their clothes. Alma and Tinna looked at each other, and began taking off their blouses. The other girls began to hesitantly take off their clothes. Liv and Anna were already running into the lake when Maria and Samantha had begun to undress. The other five girls were all properly naked and ready, but stood and waited expectantly for Maria and Samantha, cheering them on. Finally Maria and Samantha got their socks off, and carefully wriggled out of their panties, and the other girls cheered and they all ran giggling into the lake.

The lake was colder than they had hoped, and the girls stopped when the water reached up to their thighs, jumping around and hugging themselves for warmth. It didn't seem to bother Liv and Anna, who were out in the middle of it, swimming.

Alma splashed some of the cold water on Tinna. Tinna screamed, and splashed water on Alma, and the other girls all began splashing water on each other. Thalia fell in, screaming. But she didn't stand up, but let herself float, letting the clear water embrace her, slowly warming to her body. Alma and Tinna saw her float, and they looked at each other, and out to the lake, and Alma held her breath and let herself fall in, followed by Tinna.

The water was cold against their skin, that was true, but they quickly got used to it, and began swimming about, their nude forms easily gliding through the water. The other girls stood there on the shallows and watched them with awe. They were still only in up to their thighs, their pussy hovering just above the waterline.

"Come join us," Alma encouraged them, "it's only cold for a few seconds. Come swim with us."

The five girls stood there in a group and made furtive moves with their legs, but did not dare go deeper.

"You'll just get cold standing there like that," Tinna called to them.

Alma swam to Tinna, and said: "let's drag one in with us."

"Good idea. Which one?"

"The small one, Maria."

They settled on that idea, and swam to the shore. The both rose gracefully out of the lake, like a couple of water nymphs. They smiled at their friends, and headed straight at Maria, who stood beside Samantha with her arms folded. She was so short that her crotch almost touched the water where she stood. Alma and Tinna came up to her, Alma from the side, Tinna from the front, and without preamble, Tinna reached for her hand and dragged her while Alma pushed, and in a second she was submerged in the lake. The other girls reacted with screaming and tried to come to Maria's assistance, but Thalia tripped and fell, and Alma and Tinna used the opportunity to splash them all.

Two minutes later they were all swimming in the lake. Their lithe bodies slid elegantly through the cool water, and they all felt better after the first five minutes, adjusting to the temperature and the environment. They now felt cold when going out of the lake, so they stayed in the lake, swimming about. Maria and Samantha stayed where they could stand, they were now submerged up to their necks, or Maria was, the taller Samantha had her shoulders out.

The girls all returned to the shallows, and they talked and splashed water on each other.

"We forgot to bring towels," said Ingrid.

"Now you tell us," said Tove.

"We've never brought towels," said Anna, "we always just dry in the air. It only takes five minutes."

They talked more, about the school, the nuns. Sister Sara was nobody's favorite. They asked Alma how it had felt to do Sister Sara's work the other day. Alma tried to describe it, but couldn't.

"I would rather have Alma touch me than Sister Sara," said Tinna.

Maria nodded.

"Why can't we just touch each other?" asked Ingrid.

"Why does anyone even need to touch us, this is ridiculous," said Thalia.

"I don't know. You can ask the nuns. They'll say something about hygiene. At least, that's their speech every day," said Tinna.

Anna tried to emulate Sister Sara's tone: "you know girls, that cleanliness is next to Godliness. We don't use perfume to disguise or hide our body odor here."

The girls giggled.

"Why don't we just bathe in the lake always?" asked Tove. "We could bring soap."

"The nuns wouldn't have it," said Anna.

"And there aren't any hooks to hang our clothes," said Alma, eyeing their piles of clothes on the beach.

They walked out f the water up to the beach to dry themselves. As they were emerging from the water, Alma saw a face in the bushes. She peered her eyes at it, and saw that it was that pudgy boy. She had a little shock, a little shiver, knowing that she was being watched by a boy, but it was too late now to cover herself. She held eye contact with him as she rose from the water and came all the way to dry land. She saw another face, eyes glancing at her from behind a tree, and felt her face flush a little with embarrassment. And she looked around the bushes, and saw that there had to be at least four boys in there, leering at them. She touched Tinna's arm, still looking at the boys hidden in the trees, and said: "we are being watched."

Tinna glanced to the trees. She startled and covered her pussy and nipples when she saw the boys.

"It's too late for that," said Alma, and forced herself to face the boys, arms akimbo, daring them to take it all in. Her body would be jerk-off material for them for years to come.

Ingrid and Thalia came up to Alma and Tinna and asked what they were looking at, and Tinna pointed into the trees.

"The perverts!" said Ingrid.

"There are boys in the bushes watching us!" called Thalia.

Maria and Samantha, who had been walking along the beach, having a carefree conversation startled and covered themselves and ran to their clothes. They were mortified. Liv and Anna looked, saw the face, smiled and said: "let's catch them!"

And Anna and Liv ran to the bushes, and the four guys hiding there stood up and ran, and Alma and Tinna, Thalia, Ingrid and Tove all followed after them, bare-ass naked. The boys could run very fast, but they kept looking behind them and that slowed them, but the girls were nude, unencumbered by any fabric that could slow down their movement. The girls started to enjoy themselves, and giggled and screeched joyously as they ran. Alma was getting worried, because they were getting closer to the school, and she didn't know how far Anna and Liv would take their chase. If they would actually streak the grounds. But finally one of the boys tripped and fell, and Anna, who was the fastest of them, caught him.

She called out and the other girls converged on her. They surrounded Anna and the boy. Anna straddled him, holding his hands above his head. He looked around at them as they stood over him, looking down on him.

"What should we do with him?" asked Anna, with a mischievous smile.

"Let's kiss him," said Tinna. She recognized the boy. It was that pudgy boy, she had seen him naked, she remembered how embarrassed he had looked, standing there in the dressing room covering his little dick, and that made her feel easy.

The girls looked at each other, excited. The boy squirmed around a little, but Anna held him firm. She was almost seventeen, older, more muscular than he was. She was top of her class in gymnastics.

"Me first," said Anna, and she lay herself full-body on the boy, and gave him a loving kiss. He calmed down and lay silent under her. She rose from him to her elbows, looking him in the eyes, and he looked at her back, silent, calm. She kissed him again, gave him tongue, and he let her. She slowly rose up again, still straddling him, and moved his arms to his sides. She looked at the girls, and gave them a signal. The girls eyed each other, smiling, and Thalia stepped forth. She came down on all fours. They made eye contact, she and the boy, and she came from the side and gave him a kiss. Just lip to lip smooch, but she also pecked him a few times, making exaggerated kissing noises. She rose back, smiling at the boy, then stood up.

"Lift him up," said Tinna, "I don't want to crawl on the ground."

Anna and Thalia helped to raise the boy to his feet. And Tinna made sure to walk to him as sensuously as she could, swaying her hips and perking out her breasts, and she looked him all up and down before she embraced him and kissed him. She Frenched him, like Anna, but held on longer. She gave him the bedroom eyes before she backed away from him. He was breathing very heavily. The girls noticed that he was tenting, and started to point and giggle. The boy's face grew red.

Alma came next. She ran her hands down the boy's body, then lay each hand on the side of his face and kissed him with passion. She didn't stick her tongue in his mouth, but licked his lips. She backed away from him when she was done, licking her lips.

Tove was next, and she approached the boy, eyeing the erection in his pants, and she reached out to fondle him there as she pressed her body against his and kissed him. He gave a soft yelp as she fondled his member, and then licked her exploring tongue appreciatively. The girls watched with amazement and awe as they played their tongues together. And Tove let go of his member and sucked on his tongue and had it in her mouth. She left the boy looking excited, and his erection was pulsating in his pants.

Ingrid began her turn by licking the boys face. She kissed his cheeks, nibbled in his ears. She licked his lips so slowly and sensuously, then ran her tongue softly in between his lips, and they started French kissing. When she backed away she gave him a parting stroke on his male member, causing it to pulsate in his pants.

It was then Liv's turn. She stood before the boy, letting him take her all in, his member pulsating in his pants as he beheld her elegant curves; she was perky and athletic, like Anna, but slightly shorter. She looked Anna in the eye, and gave her a mischievous smile. They nodded at each other. Liv stepped up to the boy, stroked his hair, petted him on the cheek, running her hand down his face to his neck, and then lower. She gave him a soft, friendly kiss on the lips, and then she lowered herself to her knees, and she began to unzip his pants. The boy stood in silent surprise while she reached in to get out his erect male member. It was not large, probably the size of a thumb, but it was fully erect. Liv looked up at the boy, holding his penis gently in her fingers, she was giving him the bedroom look, and then her attention was on his little penis again, she fondled it lightly, then she kissed it on the tip, she licked it, she folded back the foreskin, she pulled it back, she opened her mouth and put it in, and she began moving her head back and forth on rhythmic motions, as the girls stood around, gaping with awe.

Alma gaped as she watched Liv suck the boy's penis. She'd never seen that happen before. And now she was all hot and she wanted to suck Gunnar's penis. She looked around, and saw that Tove and Ingrid were covertly touching themselves, that is, they looked like they were just covering their pussies, but she could see that their had their middle finger inside, moving, stirring about. Thalia stood beside them, and she was vigorously flicking her bean, not even bothering to hide it. Alma nudged Tinna, and pointed it out.

"You want to as well," said Tinna, nudging her.

"Ha?"

"We're all aroused, you too, just admit it."

Alma was silent. It was true. She was moist. She felt awful, and she needed release. "But here?"

"That girl is sucking a boys cock right in front of us."

The boy came, and Liv licked him clean and stood up, and she and Anna kissed him and released him.   He walked way, silently disappearing in between the trees.

6

The girls find
sexual release

Anna and Liv smiled as they saw Alma and Tinna, watching as the other three girls masturbated. They walked to Alma and Tinna and asked them: "why don't you join them?"

Ingrid and Tove looked up, and stopped masturbating and hid their hands behind their back and looked sheepish. Anna smiled at them. Thalia stroked herself unconcerned about the other girls.

"I can't, not in public," said Alma.

"Come on, we're all girls here," said Anna, stepping closer to Alma. She looked at Thalia, and Alma looked at her as well, and Anna said: "look at her, she'd doing it, she's not embarrassed in the least."

And Anna bit her tongue and she looked Alma down and up, and she looked her in the eye: "but what if you do us?"

"What do you mean?"

"What if you do your nun-thing on us. It's not like you haven't done it before. And I want to try it."

"What?"

"I want to feel how it is to have you finger me. We all know how it feels to have Sister Sara slide her fingers through our pussy, but we don't all know how it is to have you do it, and on our own volition too. I mean, it has to be better."

Thalia stopped masturbating and listened: "I like that idea," she said.

The girls looked at Thalia.

"I think you should do it Alma, I think you should touch us. I'm in if you are."

"Come on, I'll lick you if you do it for me," said Anna.

Alma gave her a doubtful look.

"Will you do it if I lick you?"

Tinna giggled. "I want to see this," she said.

Alma frowned at her.

"Just lean up against this tree here, and part your legs," said Anna, she was forcing Alma to step back. Anna was a little bit taller than Alma, all of her body a little bit bigger, wider hips and thicker thighs and bigger breasts swaying on her chest, and all that intimidated Alma. "Lean here," said Anna, and she helped Alma lean against the tree, and Alma allowed Anna to spread her legs. The girls stood around, looking curious and excited.

Anna doubled her legs under her and leaned in between Alma's thighs, face to pussy, and she gave her labia a soft lick. She looked around at the other girls: "the rest of you could all do this." The girls looked at each other. Anna turned and licked Alma's pussy again. Alma stood and stared open-mouthed into the tree-crowns as Anna licked her slit like an ice-cream. There was no hesitation in her, she just licked, running her soft yet firm tongue deep between Alma's labia and across her clit, then wriggled it on her clit, and kissed it, biting it between her lips and blowing on it, then licking it again. Alma looked down, and saw that Thalia, Liv and Tove were engaged in a tree-way kiss, their hands down fondling in each other's vaginas. Tinna and Ingrid were in full, passionate embrace, sampling each other's saliva, feeling the texture of each other's tongue. Anna was using her fingers now, massaging Alma's clit and her inner labia from the inside as she licked the same from the outside. Alma's brain fogged with pleasure and her eyes rolled back in their sockets. Anna's tongue was very dextrous, and she could really work Alma's clit with it, wrap around it and slide it through. And Alma could feel herself quake from the inside, the streams of well-being surging throughout her body, shaking it, and she moaned. Anna shushed her, then began licking her again. Alma petted Anna's head as the surges of orgasms subsided, and Anna stood up, wiped her mouth with the back of her hand, and they embraced.

"Okay, I'll finger you like Sister Sara," said Alma to her, once her orgasm had subsided.

"Next time I want you to dress like her and finger all of us in the changing room."

"Oh you..."

Anna embraced Alma, kissing her, letting Alma taste of her own pussy. She leaned back with a satisfied grin, and Alma reached down and ran her finger through Anna's slit. Anna took some deep breaths, and Alma looked around as she caressed Anna's genitals. Anna was allowing her to touch her, so Alma could freely feel around more in Anna's slida, and she felt her every fold and crevice carefully and with respect. She saw Tinna and Ingrid standing, watching her and Anna, touching each other. Thalia was under Liv, and they were licking each other in the 69 position, while Tove stood back and watched, her hands behind her back. She looked satisfied.

Anna's pussy vibrated with orgasm and Alma felt a small surge of fluids from Anna as she came on her fingers, some splashed on her mons Venus and her thighs, leaking down to her own pussy. Anna's body was still quaking as she embraced Alma, and Alma let her, and they kissed, and Anna put her tongue inside Alma's mouth and they played their tongues together.

"It's getting dark, we should find out clothes and get back," said Tove.

Alma and Anna leaned away from each other, smiling faintly. "We should do this again," said Anna. Alma smiled.

They walked back to the beach.

Maria and Samantha were still there, already

dressed, guarding their clothes.

"Where were you?" asked Samantha, worried.

"We just got lost in the woods," said Alma.

The other girls nodded.

"Did you catch the boys?"

"No."

They all quietly got dressed, and walked back to the school. They made it before the nuns became suspicious.

7

The girls watch the boys skinny dipping

Alma, Tinna and Tove sneaked through the woods to the lake. They had seen some of the boys head there, and thought they could catch a glimpse of them from the usual vantage point that Anna had told them about. The girls could hear the boys as they approached them, and they hid in the bushes and peered from behind trees at the boys, as they appeared on the small beach. There were six of them, half of the unofficial school football team; Gunnar, Ulf, Lasse, Jan, Olof and Christian. The girls held back their giggles as they watched them all get undressed. The boys took it all off without hesitation, every stitch, and Tove's face became all red as she saw a penis for the first time. Then she saw six penises, all swinging about as the boys tussled on the beach, and then ran into the lake.

"Gunnar has the biggest penis," said Tove.

"I know. And they're all bigger than that David statue. That David must have had an unusually small penis."

"You know?"

"Maybe men just had smaller dicks back then," said Tinna.

The girls watched quietly as the boys swam in the lake, then Tove had an idea: "I'm going to steal their clothes."

Before Alma or Tinna could react to that, she was off, running through the woods to where the boys had left their clothes. Alma and Tinna looked at each other, and Alma decided to run after Tove: "I'm going to help her."

"Wait for me!" whispered Tinna, and she stood up and they ran crouching after Tove.

Tove got in very close, and she crawled out from the shrubs, laying as low as she could to reach the boy's clothes. They had flung them all around, on the trees and on the ground. Alma looked at the boys swimming in the lake, and smiled. They looked so athletic, so strong, so healthy. And she was pranking them again. She smiled as she plucked someone's underpants from a tree, and gathered some scattered clothes, and then she and her friends hurried back to their vantage point with their loot, softly giggling with anticipation.

They examined their loot when they came back to their vantage point: "what do we have?" asked Alma.

"I have three shorts, four socks, two pants, a shirt," said Tove, examining one of the shorts. They were white.

"I have two shorts and three pants and a shirt," said Tinna, "and some socks," she smelled one of the socks, grimaced, and dropped the whole pile on the ground.

"Then I have the rest of the shirts," said Alma, and she held up the undies that she'd plucked from a tree and looked at them. They looked clean. She smelled them, she though they smelled fine, imbued with a hint of that manly smell of penis.

"Do you think the nuns stand over them and smell them after the shower?" asked Tove.

"They don't," said Alma.

"How would you know?"

Alma and Tinna looked at each other and smiled: "we went into the boys shower before."

"Oh you did! How was it?"

"Oh it was so wonderful! Amazing!"

"How were they? Did you see their penises?"

"We saw many penises, but they covered themselves. They all looked so strong and manly."

"Alma touched Gunnar's penis," said Tinna.

Alma blushed.

"How come you haven't told me before?"

"Well, Sister Sara came in and made Tinna undress, and that was kind of humiliating..." said Alma.

"They are coming out of the water," said Tinna, interrupting her. The girls turned to look, and saw two of the boys wade out of the lake, their bodies emerging from the water to glisten in the sun. They stood on the shore and talked for a while. The girls silently watched their glistening wet bodies in the sun. They were not as muscular as David the statue, but their penises were much larger, the tips of them dangling lower than their ball-sacks. The girls felt all tingly inside.

"I wish we were closer," said Tove, not taking her eyes off them.

"We could have them chase us," said Tinna, "we have their clothes."

A third boy came out of the lake, and he passed the other two and seemed to be looking at the area where they had flung their clothes. The girls writhed in anticipation. The boy had noticed that the clothes were gone. He turned around and informed the other two boys, and they had a look, and the girls held back giggles as they saw the naked boys rummaging around in the bushes for their clothes. The three other boys came out of the lake, and they all conferred together.

Tove grabbed one of the underpants, and before the other girls could react she jumped out of her hiding place and waved at the naked boys: "we have your clothes!"

Alma and Tinna also stood up, holding some of the boy's clothes, and they danced around, waving the clothes around. The naked boys looked at them, and at each other, and they all came running. The girls jumped in glee as they saw the six boys come running toward them, all stark naked, their wet bodies glistening in the sun and their penises swinging wildly between their thighs. The turned and girls ran away and through the little woods, to the next beach and they ran as fast as they could, dropping articles of clothing as they went. The boys ignored the dropped clothes and caught up with the girls, one after another.

Jan and Christian caught Tove on the sand. She fell down and the naked boys came down and started tickling her. They started pulling off her clothes while she laughed, unable to resist. She felt her panties slide off, and relaxed as Jan unbuttoned her white shirt-blouse. Jan and Christian removed all but her socks and shoes, and when they had her exposed like that, they started to lick her body all over.

Tinna got cornered up against a tree by Ulf and Lasse and Olof. Tinna stood still, her back against that tree, red faced and open-mouthed, while those stark naked boys stood there before her, their nude bodies slick and wet, their muscles firm, their penises still hanging limp as they closed in, waiting to pounch on her.

Alma ran deeper into the woods, and was out of

sight from the others when Gunnar caught her. They fell to the ground, and he grabbed a hold on her and they squirmed until she was on her back facing him. He held her there, she was all blushing, red-faced like a boiled lobster, and he held her arms above her head and looked her in the eyes. He had such beautiful blue eyes. She knew she was stuck, and she was so turned on, having him naked on top of her. She could feel his genitalia pressing against her belly as he straddled her. She wished she could make him fuck her, and she was sure that he wanted to. He lay down on her, slowly, and she could feel his flesh rise, he lay on top of her after all, she could feel it between her thighs, through her skirt.   He moved himself into a more comfortable position, with his member cradled in her skirt, its tip gently touching her crotch. She felt herself become moist.

"Why did you steal our clothes?" he asked her.

"So that you'd be forced to walk back naked."

"What if I take your clothes and wear them instead?"

"You wouldn't."

"I would."

"I can give you your clothes back."

"Oh?"

"Let me go and I'll go and get them and give the to you, I promise."

"After I punish you."

"No!"

"Yes," he said, sliding a little forward, so that she could feel his fully erect peen plow into her crotch. She was scared, but at the same time she wanted him inside her so much.   Then she thought about Sister Sara's daily hymen inspection, and her eyes widened with panic and she exclaimed: "Wait! Wait!"

"What now?"

"I'll let you fuck me, but you have to fuck me in the ass."

He stared at her, he was thinking it over, she could see it. And he answered: "okay," and he smiled, shining his beautiful straight white teeth at her.

Alma smiled, her blood flowing, her head spinning with anticipation. Her first real sexual experience would take place out in the woods. That was so romantic. "Let me take off my panties," she said, and he let her hands go and rose from her, sitting himself in front of her, legs doubled under him, thighs spread. She rose up to a sitting position, and made a sigh as she saw his erect penis again. It was so big. She pulled up her skirt, and dragged down her panties. She had to lie down to get them off, and Gunnar helped her removing them from her feet. "Can we please do this standing up, I don't want to dirty myself more than this," she asked him, sitting in front of him.

He smiled at her and they both stood up, and he pointed and told her: "get up against this tree, and hold on to it while I stick it in."

She looked, and saw a tree some meters behind her. She looked at him and asked: "can I hold your penis on the way?"

Gunnar nodded to her, smiling, and he let her hold his penis while they walked to the tree. She felt the surge of satisfaction a she held his peen in her hand, it was so thick and warm and so soft yet so firm. She let him go when she came to the tree and she took a wide stance and hugged the tree, and she leaned herself into it, so her ass stood out toward Gunnar. And she felt as Gunnar lifted her skirt, exposing her ass, and she closed her eyes as she felt the tip of his peen slide along her crack, slowly entering the crack. Gunnar's penis was between her ass-cheeks like a hot-dog in a bun as he reached around her, and holding one arm around her waist he got one hand in between her thighs, stroking her pussy. She shook with anticipation, knowing that his peen was as thick as it was, and just hoped it wouldn't hurt her too much as he forced it in her ass. He clumsily stroked her labia while he poked at her ass with his penis, trying to find her hole. She tried not to clench, taking deep breaths to relax. After a few pokes he found her ass-hole, and began working his way in. That felt super-uncomfortable to Alma, and she had to really concentrate to relax her ass-hole to let him in. He was twisting and pushing, forcing her hole open, slowly expanding it. Alma took deep breaths to relax her sphincter, she felt like she was passing an enormous dump as he entered her. But he got his penis inside her ass, and he could concentrate more on fingering her pussy while he slowly fucked her from behind. Alma was cross-eyed, she felt like she was being masturbated while pooping. Nobody had told her this was how it felt. The tree was cold and uncomfortable, and she considered trying this again some other place, somewhere more comfortable, like in a bed. But she had Gunnar's penis inside her, and that was all that mattered. He was masturbating her, and that was nice of him, she thought. His penis was a little bit uncomfortably long, she thought. She believed it really should have entered her vagina, but then Sister Sara would have done unspeakable things to her when she inevitably found out. Like that girl she had seen once that hadn't passed the inspection. Sister Sara had taken her with her and she had stayed in with the nuns for the weekend, and when she came back she never said a word again. So Gunnar's thick and long penis in her ass would be okay for until she graduated. Gunnar came inside her as she was thinking these things, and she felt him push even harder inside her, and pause. He let out a sigh and he embraced her from behind, gently stroking her belly and fondling her breasts, and then he dragged himself out. And it really felt to her like she was pooping.

"Oh shit!" she heard him say. And she felt more come out of her, she heard it make wet sticky noises on the ground as it hit it, and she felt embarrassed. He laughed. She dropped her skirt back down and turned around, red faced, careful not to step in her own droppings. His peen was smeared with her feces. She frowned.

"We'll do this again, but next time, after you have gone to the toilet," he said. She felt embarrassed, but she felt more easy at hearing him say that. That meant he wanted to fuck her again, and that meant that he could be her boyfriend.

"Let's go find your clothes."

They walked through the woods holding hands, she still holding her panties in her other hand. They found Ulf standing naked by a tree, watching something, his member firm. He heard them come from behind, turned to look at them, and smiled as he saw them, pointing at what he was looking at. And they stood beside Ulf and they saw Tinna on her knees, sucking Lasse's member. Olof stood beside them, his member firm and erect in his hand.

"She already did me," said Ulf, and he looked at

them and he asked: "what were you doing?"

Alma bit her lower lip as she lifted her skirt, flashing her pussy to Ulf.

"You didn't..." and he saw Gunnar's member, "is that shit on your dick?"

Gunnar nodded.

"You fucked her in the ass! Oh, man, you the man!" and they fist-bumped, and then they hugged. "I'm so proud of you!" he said, and they stepped back, and he sighed and said: "you put some of Alma's shit on me."

Lasse came, and Tinna licked him off and he backed away. He waved to Alma and the boys, and they walked toward him. Tinna and Olof also looked at them, and waved, but Olof poked Tinna, and she turned back. Without preamble, she started sucking Olof's penis.

"Gunnar fucked Alma in the ass," said Ulf.

"You did? You the man," said Olof, and he and Gunnar shook hands and hugged.

Alma got turned on seeing those nude men keep hugging each other. She noticed that they were both hard, and had to ask: "aren't you uncomfortable doing that?"

"What do you mean?"

"I mean, ah... never mind," she said dismissively, and enjoyed the view.

And she listened as they talked about fucking while they watched Tinna suck Olof's cock. It didn't take long for them to finish, and then Alma and Tinna got the pleasure of seeing Olof hug Gunnar, their erect penises touching. Tinna looked down between Gunnar's thighs, bit her lip and winked him. Then they all went to look for Tove.

They found Tove and Jan and Christian all lying naked together on the beach. Jan and Christian lay on their backs, while Tove lay spread out on top of them, sucking Jan's peen while pumping Christian's sex organ manually with her hand. When Tove saw her friends arrive, she startled, jumped to her feet and covered herself with her hands. Jan and Christian reacted more calmly, and rose to their feet to greet them, their members still erect. And they were still erect when Ulf told them about Gunnar's fucking of Alma, and Alma got to see her nude boyfriend hugged by another nude male with an erection. It almost made her feel jealous.

"We should all go swimming," said Ulf.

The others liked that, and Alma and Tinna looked at each other, and they both started to undress. They threw off their blouses, and the boys cheered as the girls dropped their skirts. Alma didn't need to take off her panties, but she still had on her top, which she quickly took off and flung away. And off flew their shoes, and their socks, and the girls stood nude with the boys. Alma and Tinna stood proudly, arms akimbo as they looked around, at the boys, at Tove. They smiled at Tove, standing there looking so embarrassed with two nude boys to the left of her and two nude boys to the right of her, erections subsiding.

"I wish I had my camera," said Tinna.

"Let's swim," said Alma.

And they ran into the lake and swam.

8

Rendez-vois
in the washroom

Alma and Gunnar began seeing each other more. They would disappear into the woods, hold hands and talk about their future and their feeling and kiss. They could stand up against a tree and kiss for hours, or so they felt, feeling each other's lips, tasting each other's tongue. Sometimes they would sit or lie in a clearing, and Alma would let Gunnar feel her breasts, or run his hands down her panties and twirl his fingers on her clit. It felt nice, and Gunnar seemed to like doing it. Alma liked to reward him for masturbating her, so she unzipped his fly and reached in with her hand. He grew quickly as she sought him, and he was fully enlarged when she got him out. His peen was all large and veiny, and she liked to stroke it, to feel it's velvety skin on her hands. She leaned down and kissed the tip, touching it with her tongue, and feeling doubtful about being able to fit him in her mouth, she jerked him off. She caught his splooge in her hand, and tasted it before she wiped it up with her Cleenex. The decided to have sex again, but not out in the open. Someone might come and see them. They could hear others in the woods.

"We could do it in the wash-room," said Alma, "after midnight. The nuns always go to sleep early. I'll stay awake and let you in."

Gunnar agreed to that, and they plotted their meeting in more detail before parting. And so it was that Gunnar showed up at the girl's dorm at midnight. He didn't have to wait, as Alma was waiting for him at the door, and she let him in, and she led him to the wash-room. The wash-room was where the nuns and the girls who had drawn the lots that week washed their laundry. There were four washing machines and four dryers, and stacks of laundry on shelves, both school uniforms and nun habits. The whole room was dry and warm and smelled of detergent.

"I brought Vaseline," said Alma, "do you want

me to apply it?"

Gunnar said nothing, just embraced her and kissed her. He kissed her on the cheek and nibbled on her ear, and then he kissed her neck all over, softly but with passion, nibbling her a little as he ran his hands down her back, grasping her ass cheeks and holding her against him. She could feel his male member rising. He lifted her by her thighs and sat her on one of the washing machines, still kissing her, and he felt her up and found that she was bare assed. He stepped back, holding up her skirt and looked down on her softly furry pussy as she spread her legs for him. He crouched down and put his face between her thighs and blew delicately on her fur. He blew on her clit, and came in closer, and poked her clit with his tongue, played with it a little, touched his nose against it, he put his nose in her slit and ran it up, following with his tongue, and he licked her again and again, first just her vaginal lips, her outer labia, then he pushed inside her slit, gently caressing her floppy meat with his tongue. He leaned back, and just beheld the wonderful beauty of her femininity, then looked up into her eyes, and said: "let's fuck."

Alma opened her little can of Vaseline, and Gunnar undid his pants so she could sensuously smear some of the lubricant on his penis. She spread much of it, remembering how it had felt when he fucked her in the ass in the woods. Satisfied with her handy-work, she stood up, propped herself against the washing machine and spread her legs. Gunnar stepped up to her and lifted her skirt, revealing the smooth orbs of her firm, wide feminine ass. Alma bent over on the washing machine, and she felt as Gunnar's member touched her between her cheeks and was slowly being pushed in, exploring her crack. He was slowly guiding himself with his hand, and he found her hole and gently bored his male member into it. All lubed up, he entered her much more easily, and he fucked her more gently. It was as intimate a feeling as Alma had remembered it being, but less painful. She lamented the size of his male member, as gentle as Gunnar was fucking her, his penis was too big to fit her ass-hole. It still hurt, but she felt loved. She looked forward to leaving the school, so she could make Gunnar fuck her in her pussy. The thought made her feel warm inside as he pumped her.

Gunnar had just come, and was pulling up his pants when the door came open and two persons came in. Alma and Gunnar startled and looked at the pair, and they in returned gave them a wide-eyed surprised look.

"Tove!" Alma gasped.

"Alma!" Tove gasped.

Gunnar breathed lighter, and the boy that Tove had brought with her did too. Tova was relieved.

"What are you doing here?"

Tove looked at the two of them, and replied calmly: "the same thing as you did, I think."

"Oh... do you want to borrow my Vaseline?"

Tove and the boy looked at each other, then said: "yes please."

"I told you we should have used the showers," said the boy, who they now saw was Jan.

"The showers?" said Gunnar, "we should got here, we can all go there together and talk while you two fuck each other and I wash my dick."

Tove and Jan looked at Gunnar's dirt-smeared member, which was still hanging out for all to see. They smiled and nodded.

"Good, that's settled," said Gunnar, dropping his pants, happy to not have to smear Alma's fecal matter on his undies, as he'd have had to do had the visitor been one of the nuns. He took off the rest of his clothes, folded them and put them on top of the washing machine Alma had leaned up against, and went naked with the three of them to the girl's changing room where the showers were. Tove and Jan entered the changing room, but Gunnar paused outside and stopped Alma: "let's fuck out here in the hallway."

Alma shrugged, she looked at him, and saw that his male organ had risen again. Without a word she faced the wall, and he lifted her skirt again and entered her, much easier now that he was lubed up and Alma's ass hadn't closed back up fully. He reached around her with his hands and enthusiastically rubbed her clit. He jerked her from the wall, and began walking her to the changing room door, his member still fully inside her. She giggled as she pushed the door open, and they entered, he still pumping her in the ass as they walked.

Tove and Jan were in there, kissing and undressing each other. They gave Alma and Gunnar a brief look and a smile, then continued getting each other naked, fondling each other gracefully. Gunnar pulled himself out of Alma so that she could take off her skirt and her blouse and her socks, the only articles of clothing that she wore, and he took off his socks, the only articles of clothing that he wore, and they entered the showers, she first, swaying her hips erogenously at him, and him following pointing at her with his erection. Alma picked a shower, turned it on and Gunnar came to her, and she ran her fingers down the sides of his body, looking him playfully in the eye. She was moist and yearned to have him thrust himself inside her pussy, but she knew the repercussions, and she crouched down, doubling her legs under her and she began washing his erect penis. She used both hands and a lot of lathered soap, and she was thorough with him, even lathering his balls. Smiling, she pumped him with her hand, looking directly into the slit of his tip. And then he came in her face, and his splooge tasted all soapy to Alma, who spit it out, laughing. She tested her handy-work by giving his cock-shaft a few licks. She turned the shower off, and pressed most of the water from her hair with her hands before the two of them exited the shower. Tove and Jan were naked on the floor, Tove on all fours while Jan pumped her from behind, doggy style, both with a pained frown on their face.

Alma leaned against the wall, crossing her arms, and asked Gunnar: "do you think we look like that when we're fucking?"

"Probably," said Gunnar. "Let's go back to the wash-room and make out."

Alma picked up her clothes, and she followed Gunnar to the wash room, where they sat naked on the washing machines and talked. An hour later Tove and Jan showed up too, but dressed, and they all talked together, until one by one, they fell asleep.

9

The boy's adventure disguised as nuns

Alma came to with the sun shining in her eye through one of the windows high on the wall. She rubbed her eyes and looked around. She was still naked in Gunnar's arms, covered in some dry towels, and she could see Tove sleeping near by in Jan's embrace, looking very loving and comfortable. Suddenly Alma became very alarmed: "It's morning!" she exclaimed, and began waking Gunnar up: "hurry, you got to get dressed! I am supposed to be in the dorm! It's time for the shower! The nuns will be in here soon! Quick! We have to get dressed!"

"Okay. I'll get dressed," said Gunnar, not looking as alarmed as Alma thought he should be.

"No! What if they see you? Boys aren't allowed in the girl's dormitory!"

"I just sneak out... they won't see me."

"No! You'll have to put on a disguise!" Alma was gathering her clothes, and putting them on in a hurry. Tova and Jan were slowly coming to.

"What's wrong?" asked Tove, and almost immediately she remembered: "shit! It's morning and we're not in bed!" and she sprung up. She pointed at Jan: "you have to get out of here! Quick!"

"No! They'll recognize him!" Alma called out to her, worried.

"How then can the leave?"

"They can put on nun-habits. Look, there are lots of nun-habits here," said Alma, pointing to a stack of nun-clothes.

"You have this all thought out," said Tove, looking at the nun-habits.

The girls helped the boys put on the nun-habits, and straightened them out.

"You look good," said Alma, "now just remember to walk slowly, like the nuns do, and nobody will ever be the wiser."

And Alma and Tove ran as softly as they could to their rooms. Alma got in and found Tinna just getting out of bed. "Where have you been?"

Tinna asked.

"Doing what I told you about yesterday," said Alma, with a mischievous smile.

"Oh, you cheeky..."

Alma found her panties and put them on, then she took off her blouse and her skirt, and she took a few deep breaths to calm herself down before she left the bedroom with Tinna.

The girls all slowly gathered in the changing room as they did every morning, and waited for Sister Sara and her helpers. Sister Sara arrived as the last girls filed in, followed by two nuns. Alma didn't pay them much mind at first, then she saw their faces: it was Gunnar and Jan, in their nun-disguises. Alma's eyes grew to double their size but she kept quiet. How had this happened? Hadn't Sister Sara noticed who she picked up from the halls? Was she blind? Tove had noticed too, and came to Alma and poked her in the arm, whispering agitated as she pointed: "look, it's them!"

"Shut up!" Alma whispered back through her teeth. "If she notices we're doomed."

"But... we can't let them be in here."

"We have to. This is our fault. Now shut up

and act normal."

The girls began undressing, taking off their shirts, exposing their lithe bodies and smooth skin, and sliding off their panties, one and two and three at a time, and their perky asses and fluffy pubes came to view, and they piled their clothes as usual. Alma and Tove undressed as they always did, eyeing the boys. Their faces were growing red. Alma wondered what would happen if any of the other girls would notice. She hoped that she'd not cry out, and if she did, the boys would just be blamed for perversion on their own. She'd make it up to them somehow.

The girls didn't look at the new nuns, they just stood around casually as always, in the nude, chatting inanely while the first batch filed into the shower. Sister Sara waved the boys to come, and had them stand guard at the shower room doorway while she tended to something else. And the boys stood there and literally drooled as they beheld all the beautiful nude bodies all glistening wet under the warm, gentle streams, all softly running their hands all over their bodies, lathering themselves, getting clean before inspection. And as usual, some girls stood in the doorway, totally nude with the people they thought were just nuns, and watched the girls showering along with them. The boys thanked heavens for that the habits were voluminous as they were, for they had risen to their fullest extent from enjoying the view. The girls were still ignoring them, being used to be watched over in the shower by nuns.

The first batch of heavenly bodies exited the shower, still ignoring the boys, even though they dispensed towels to them after the showers, the girls just received their towels without even looking at who was handing them out and they dried themselves before the second batch entered the showers. Alma and Tove were with them, and they both struggled not to cover their privates with their hands as they passed them, but they still felt hot in the face, knowing that they were being watched by two boys. Alma felt very conscious of her bare ass as she walked away from them and into the shower room. Alma didn't mind Gunnar seeing her naked, but Jan was another matter entirely. The same went for Tove. Tinna was also in the second batch, and she noticed, and she leaned over and whispered to Alma while they were showering: "I think one of those nuns is a boy."

"They both are. That's Gunnar and Jan. Don't tell anyone."

Tinna looked at the nuns, she looked them in the eyes, and she saw that they were indeed Gunnar an Jan. And she smiled, blushing, "you have to tell me all about it later," she said, and she shook her head, and she was silent.

Alma felt so embarrassed at having to wash her slit in front of her boyfriend and his friend. The shame! But she knew she had to, or else she'd have to shower again, and be humiliated even more. She faced the wall as she lathered the soap and tried not to think about the boys as she spread out her crotch and rubbed her slit clean, and she couldn't help but think about what she was doing, now that the boys were watching her do it. The other girls didn't know to face the wall like she did. If they knew... She was extra thorough, washing herself. She glanced at Tinna, and hoped that she wasn't masturbating, because it looked like she was. She was facing the doorway, it was suspicious. Was that silly girl playing for the audience? Suddenly it occurred to Alma that she might look even more like she was masturbating than had she just faced away from the wall. But she felt really exposed as it was, and spreading her pussy at the boys felt too much. She glanced at the boys, they looked overwhelmed by what they were seeing. Girls were spreading their pussies for them. It was for cleaning, but they saw more vagina than they ever had before. The second batch of girls left the shower room all slick wet and clean, breasts jiggling, and Alma and Tove tried not to notice the boys as they passed between them, nude as they were and red-faced. And they just barely withstood the temptation, no: urge to cover their sex. The boys got a good look at their exposed nude bodies, from head to toe, Alma was sure. Tinna smiled and winked at the boys. The boys handed out the towels, and only Alma, Tove and Tinna thought to look them in the face as they received them, exchanging knowing glances. Alma took some slight comfort in being temporarily covered by the towel while she watched as the third group entered the showers, hips swaying, their small, perky asses jiggling like jelly.

Sister Sara had taken the time to line up all the clean underwear for the girls for them to put on once she had done molesting them again. The girls were beginning to get into place, positioning themselves to have their conversations where they would fall into line. When Alma and her friends had dried themselves and reluctantly returned their towels to the boys, Sister Sara began lining the girls up. She took her time, knowing that the last batch of girls would be in the showers for at least five minutes. The boys looked away from the girls cleaning their vagina in the shower to see the growing lines of bare female bottoms. They had been hard for more than ten minutes, their erect members rubbing constantly against the fabric of their undies, stimulating them, they could feel the precum wetting their undies. They felt a yearning to stick their members in between one of those ass-cheeks and pump some.

The last batch exited she shower, a dozen girls. They had been in such a high spirits that they could share showers. They sometimes did, but it was rare. The nuns liked it, because it took less time to shower three batches. There were only ten towels, so two girls waited, arms crossed under their ample breasts, as if emphasizing them.   And as they waited, they noticed something about those two nuns, first one, who then pointed it to the other, and they made a face, an expression of shock and amusement, and they blushed. And they dried themselves, stealing glances at the boys, then staring, smiling, ashamed of their nudity but intrigued by what they were seeing.

The girls were all lined up, and Sister Sara pointed the boys to come to her where she stood at one end of the line. The boys looked at each other, and they took their time walking between the lines of nude girls, taking in the sight of all those girl's bare backsides on one side, those softly curved crevices, those well shaped moons, and on the other side the array of soft breasts and softly fluffy pussies. They came to the end of the line, where they turned and slowly walked between the next lines and enjoyed the front view of all the girls they'd just seen the backsides of, those shapely chest-mounds, some perky, some drooping, and those well shaped mons, while resisting the temptation to touch the bare bottoms on the other side. Sara watched them as they took their time, nodding approvingly. She'd never seen the nuns so involved in their work before.

Sister Sara told Gunnar to stay with her, following her with a towel, while Jan had to walk the line again, and wait on the other end, which he did gladly. For what reason he had to do this he didn't ask, he just walked slowly past the front-most line, taking in the girl's natural beauty again. He paused to look up Alma and Tinna, because hadn't they come into the boy's shower the other day to look at him? Alma and Tinna stood as frozen, hands by their sides, while he leered lasciviously at them, their uncovered bodies, taking in their soft bush, their feminine curves, their perky, youthful breasts. He winked at Tove, Tove blushed. The two red-faced girls who had discovered him watched him with awe as he walked by. He walked to the end, and turned around, where he could see the arrays of pussies and titties, and wished he could masturbate to relieve himself of his nearly unendurable horniness.

"Hands down by your sides," said Sister Sara.

She didn't have to this time, as the girls all stood straight and with their hands limp by their sides, their private features exposed to Sara's view, but she was a creature of habit. She moved to a point where she could see them all, and looking at them from one side to the other, just admiring their shape and the cleanness of their nude bodies, she said: "look at you, all looking so clean and dry. So young, so beautiful."

This was the first time Alma didn't get the creeps by Sister Sara's pre-inspection speech. She was just too embarrassed, knowing about the two boys watching her standing there naked. She saw Gunnar stood by the end of the line, holding a towel. She wondered how embarrassed she'd be had they not been having sex earlier. Thinking about that made her feel a little better.

"You know girls, that cleanliness is next to Godliness," said Sister Sara, continuing her speech, "we don't use perfume to disguise or hide our body odor here."

Sister Sara walked back to the end of the line, and turned to face the first girl, telling her: "arms up," and the girl raised her arms. "Turn around please, slowly," said Sister Sara, and the girl turned around slowly while Sara and Gunnar feasted their eyes on her beautiful exposed body, taking in her nudity, appreciating her. The girl stopped turning, facing Sister Sara, and Sara ran her hands down her arms and through her armpit-fur, and the girl rested her hands on the top of her head as Sister Sara leaned in holding her by the waist and smelled her armpits, and she smiled with approval and she looked down on the girl's beautiful furry pussy. Sister Sara smiled as she stroked the girl's pussy gently, then running her finger through her slit, feeling between her labia, stimulating her clit just a little. The girl shook a little, as always when Sister Sara did this to her. She was used to it, she expected it. Sister Sara brought her finger up to her face and smelled it, nodded with approval, smiled at the naked girl, Gunnar handed Sara the towel to dry her finger on, and she moved to the next girl. That meant that Gunnar stood right in front of the naked girl that Sister Sara had just fingered, and they looked each other in the eye. The girl saw Gunnar, and recognized him, and he smiled at her. Suddenly deeply embarrassed, the naked girl grew red faced when she realized that she was naked with a boy, but didn't dare let out a sound. She stood motionless, dared do nothing else, hands on top of her head as always, becoming red-faced.

The next girl in line was pudgy little Maria, and Maria turned around while sister Sara ran her eyes over her skin, front and back. And pudgy Maria saw Gunnar, and a cold stream of embarrassment and shame ran down her back as she recognized him, and she looked at Sister Sara and then at Gunnar, and she believed that this was as it should be, since Sara was perfectly calm, and so was the girl beside her, but she looked away from him, and didn't dare make eye contact. Maria winced a little when Sister Sara fingered her pussy, and she swallowed hard and tried not to look at Gunnar. Maria's friend Samantha was also shocked at seeing Gunnar while she was as nude and as uncovered as she thought she could possibly be, and she looked at her friend beside her, wide eyed with astonishment, then at Gunnar, and couldn't take her eyes off him, even when Sister Sara ran her finger through her labia.

Sister Sara thought it a little strange how wet her finger was after running it through Samantha's slit; usually, with a few exceptions, the girls were more dry. She touched her again, fondling her clit and hooking her middle finger inside her, she motioned around inside her slida, and found that she was moist. Sister Sara licked her fingers, and tasted nothing abnormal, and tried again, twirling her fingers on Samantha's slick and slippery clit while thinking about why that girl might be so wet. Samantha's eyes were rolling back in their sockets, her mouth was open, she was gasping. Sister Sara tasted Samantha's pussy juice again, thinking, then she shrugged it off, the girl's pussy was clean, that was what mattered.

Samantha felt like a new woman, having been masturbated in such a manner while looking Gunnar in the eye, both ashamed to the core and deeply turned on. Gunnar gave her such a friendly look too when he was drying Sara's fingers, and she felt that she wanted him. She could feel his eyes on her body.

Thalia raised an eyebrow in surprise when she

saw that the nun was Gunnar, and she glanced over to Jan, and she quickly recognized him. She rolled her eyes and shook her head, and decided to have a talk with Alma about this later, since she was the prime suspect in this case. Sister Sara had no criticism to make about Thalia's pussy, so she moved on to Alma. Alma made like she didn't notice Gunnar. She quietly raised her arms and turned around as normal, and she closed her eyes when Sister Sara fingered her, giving a little involuntary hiss as Sara stimulated her clit. Tinna smiled, eyeing Gunnar both before and after her little turn, but other than that she tried to remain calm and collected. Sister Sara gave her a hymen check, and she yelped softly and giggled, causing Sister Sara to frown with disapproval.

The red faced girls came next, they were writhing with anticipation, so much that Sara noticed, and she asked them: "why are you so agitated?"

"Oh, nothing, we're just excited to be here," said the first girl, and giggled.

"It is good that you're enjoying yourselves," said Sister Sara, and had her turn around, smelled her armpits and fingered her. The girl was dripping wet, and Sister Sara wondered about that. She looked the girl in the eyes, peering her eyes at her to see her better, and saw that she was smiling, biting her lips, looking at her friend. Sister Sara was suspicious, dried her fingers and went to the next girl, and had her turn around, smelled her, and ran her fingers between her labia, finding her slit dripping wet.

"You two share a room, don't you?" she asked them.

The girls said yes to that, and nodded.

Sister Sara made a mental note to herself, to report their lesbian tendencies to the Mother Superior.

Sister Sara and Gunnar moved to the next line, the middle line, and the corner girl actually paled when she noticed that Gunnar was not a nun, but a boy, feeling her privacy violated, and she looked around, and wondered why none of the other girls were reacting to him. Sara had to tell her twice to turn around, so shocked was she, and then she covered her sex out of shame, which annoyed Sara even more. Sara manually moved her hands to her sides. She had a very lovely outie, a delectable piece of roast-beef coming from between her outer labia, that Sister Sara had a habit of rubbing between her fingers and thumb. The girl had always felt awkward about that, but now that a boy was watching her nude body while Sister Sara handled her dangling roast-beef curtain, she felt mortified. Her embarrassment and shame when Sister Sara tugged on her exposed inner labia for her own amusement in front of that boy was beyond measure. Sister Sara enjoyed handling outies, and this was the most prominent and best outie in the whole lineup. She always handled this girl little bit longer, always until she was well moist, secretly fantasizing about nibbling on her. Sara smelled her hand and liked it, and Gunnar helped dry her hand and they moved to the next one. Gunnar looked at the girl, and felt sorry for her as she stood before him, tears streaming from closed eyes as she stood naked before him, clearly mortally embarrassed, her body fully exposed to him with her hands on the top of her head. He wished he could hug her to comfort her, but that would have revealed him.

Anna was next in line, she was one of the best

endowed girls in the school. She had the widest hips, but one girl had larger breasts, but that girl was also very rotund. When Anna saw that a boy was looking at her in the nude, she smiled, blushing as she did, winked at him, and moved her hands to the back of her head and stretched them back to perk out her breasts more, to better show off her sexy body. She proudly turned around when asked by Sara, slower than usual, so as to present the boy a better view of her, and then waited with anticipation for Sara to slide her finger between her labia.

She held her gaze on Gunnar's eyes as he stood in front of her while Sara had her attention on testing the next girl, and she bit her ower lip, giving him the bedroom eyes as she lowered her right arm down to her slit, she slowly started to masturbate in front of him. Gunnar stared at her, awed, and full of appreciation, his erection noticeable even through his nun-habit.

Tove shyly averted her eyes from Gunnar and smiled modestly when her turn came, and she blushed a little. The girl beside her was red-faced like a tomato, and wanted to cover her face, but didn't dare, because Sister Sara was there.

Ingrid smiled and shook her head, blushing some. The large breasted fat girl beside her nearly fainted. The next three reacted with varying levels of shock and discomfort, feeling very ashamed and exposed and violated.

Liv's turn came, and she looked pleasantly surprised at seeing the boy, and she licked her lips erogenously and gave him her bedroom-look. Then she presented herself, like Anna, and smiled. There came a soft sigh from behind Gunnar, as Anna had her orgasm. Sister Sara looked, but briefly, and determining that nothing was awry in that direction, she continued her work.

The rest of the nude girls noticed Gunnar one after another. The two at the end had already noticed Jan for what he was, but hadn't dared mention it. After all Sister Sara had brought the boys, for what reason they did not know. He smiled at them and tried to look casual, they blushed. They were all embarrassed to some degree, some more than others, some ashamed as well. Sister Sara didn't notice that the girls all blushed, some red faced like tomatoes, and declared them all clean and congratulated them for their hygiene. And she left, ordering those boy-nuns to follow her.

When Sara and the boys had left, the nude girls all stood and looked uncomfortably at each other. Anna and Liv suggested that they should masturbate, to get the feeling of embarrassment and shame out of their system. Some of them did, right then and there. They stood there and twirled their fingers on their clits. A few went back into the showers again, feeling violated, to clean themselves better. Some of the girls hurried to get their clothes on and leave, red faced and embarrassed. Alma and Tinna and Tove were among the ones who stood and flicked their bean. They felt it was very therapeutic. Afterwards, they felt much more intimate with the girls who stood with them, masturbating. The girls who hurried out and the girls who went back to the showers were very quiet in the days that followed.

10

An encounter
in the woods

Alma and Gunnar went into the woods, being careful to see if they were being followed as they disappeared into the trees. They tried to keep clear of all the other couples that went into the woods, but they inevitably saw glimpses of some, as they carelessly embraced and kissed behind near-by trees, or actually participated in oral sex. After that last episode in the dressing room, the girls all seemed to have become more sexual, somehow. Alma and Gunnar saw a boy standing up against a tree in the distance, being sucked like that by one of the girls, too far away to be identified, and they smiled at each other and did not bother them. They went deeper into the woods.

"We must not sleep in the wash-room again," said Alma.

"But that was fun."

"I bet it was, for you. How did you get to be with Sister Sara in there in the girl's changing room anyway?"

"Just, me and Jan were dressed up as those nuns, really convincing apparently, and Sister saw us and called us to come with her. We didn't dare to argue or run, so we just did as she said. We never thought we'd get to go look at all your friends naked. And that thing that Sara does, touching your pussy, do the nuns do that to you every day?"

"Oh yes, every day. Except one week a month when we have our periods."

"I swear, she masturbated at least two girls in there."

Alma nodded.

"And then we hurried away, and got rid of those nun-habits in the boy's dorm and then we just went to our rooms and jerked off. And wow... we needed that."

"Really?"

"Really. That was so hot. All those pussies, I wanted to fuck all of them. They all looked so embarrassed."

"Some of those girls are beside themselves with shame. They won't show their faces."

"Tell them to not be ashamed. They are beautiful, we wished we could fuck them all."

Alma punched Gunnar in the arm. He laughed.

"You want to kiss?"

Alma nodded. They embraced as they stood there, and Alma closed her eyes as their lips met. They stood there in the woods, out of sight from everyone and just kissed, rubbing their soft lips together, running their hands up and down each others back and sides. That was so cozy. Mild streams of pleasure ran though Alma's body. They began running their tongues against each other's lips, tongues touching from time to time as they danced around on the forest floor. She could feel his male member touching her, it had risen, and was pressing between them, sandwiched as they stood, grabbing each other's ass. She undid his belt, and he was fondling with her panty-string. But she was in a better situation for doing that, and his pants fell, and she pushed away from him and got down on her knees. She caught his penis from behind the cloth, pulling it through one of the leg-holes, and she held it firmly and pushed so that the foreskin folded away from the tip, exposing it, all red and shiny and firm, and she started licking it. She licked it like a lollipop. She kissed it sensuously, sucked it gently from one side, then the other, then from the front, licking the front slit on it, tasting the pre-cum. She could only just fit it in her mouth, as it was so thick and long, and her teeth touched it as it touched the roof of her mouth. She had to admit that his penis was uncomfortably large for this sex act, and she was beginning to look forward to having vaginal penetration sex. She had heard that she was in an enviable position for that, having such a well endowed boyfriend to fuck her, to fill up her vagina. But that was for the future, when they'd get steady, and find work, and start thinking about children. She winced as he came inside her mouth. She could feel that sticky stuff cling to the roof of her mouth. She licked his peen clean, and then took some time to lick the inside of her mouth. She swallowed all of it, wanting to keep a part of Gunnar inside her.

"Now I do you," said Gunnar, and he got down

on his knees in front of her, and he carefully lay Alma on her back. He removed her panties, flinging them over his shoulder, and pushed her legs apart, exposing her slit, spreading her labia to view. He crawled in between her legs, looking attentively into the many folds of her spread pussy as she leaned back on her haunches and watched him. He looked at her pussy, admiring it's gleaming moistness, ran his fingers through her pubes, touched her slit. He blew on her, softly, coming ever closer. He started licking her, he had enthusiasm, but not practice. Alma found herself wondering if Sister Sara could give him lessons. Sister Sara had been really good to her. Sister Sara was really good at licking pussy. But Alma let Gunnar go at her down there, giving him some hints and tips as he enthusiastically gnawed at her vagina. This was sweet of him, but he really needed practice. Alma felt confident that he would get better with practice, he seemed willing. And she looked down on him, stroking his hair as she looked forward to many years of sex with him.

"We should do it in your room," she said, when he was finished and lay beside her.

"Do what? Fuck?"

"Yes. Then I could jump out the window in the morning, and slip into my bedroom before anyone was the wiser."

"My room is on the third floor."

"Oh..."

"I could get a rope ladder."

Alma laughed: "what if I fall? Nothing suspicious going on there, just a girl coming from the boys sleeping quarters."

"If you go out early enough, nobody would be around, I guess. But you'd have to be up pretty early."

"How early?"

"We wake up the same time as you girls. So I guess an hour, half-hour before bell. But you realize that I share a room with Fleming, I don't think he'd like it if you showed up and we had loud sex while he was trying to sleep."

"What if I bring a girl for him? I mean, I know that Tinna likes Fleming. She'd totally fuck him while we were fucking."

"A double date? Okay, if you think she'll be okay with it."

"But Fleming?"

"Fleming will fuck any girl that shows up. I promise."

Alma thought about it. "I'll do it. I want to do it. I want to sleep with you bad enough to do this."

Gunnar leaned over to her and they kissed.

11

Alma and Tinna
go into the boys dorm

Alma and Tinna sneaked out of their dorm just before midnight, and sneaked toward the boys dorm. Gunnar was waiting for them by the door, as he had promised, and Fleming was with him. Tinna was more happy to see Fleming than any of them had anticipated, she embraced him like he was a lover she'd not seen for long, and gave him a wet kiss on the cheek. They all sneaked as silently as they could up to the third floor, where Gunnar and Fleming had their bedroom.

The girls jumped on the boys and kissed them as they were closing the door, and they were all writhing in their respective lover's arms, body against body, arms passing up and down, thighs grabbed, asses pinched, tongues wrestling. The boys started taking off their shirts, throwing them on the floor. The girls helped them undoing their belts, and their pants slid down, and up went their undershirts as the girls slid down their underpants.

The girls paused and backed away to behold the boys in their full naked glory. They were both athletic and strong, Fleming more muscular and defined, but Gunnar a bit taller, and his penis was longer in its limp state, and thicker across.

Alma looked at Fleming's penis, and she found herself imagining how much better it would have been to have that much smaller dick in her ass, and it would fit in her mouth too. Meanwhile Tinna was awed by Gunnar's cock, not having experienced it up her ass. Alma looked at Tinna, and might as well be reading her thoughts.

"Let's get you boys up," said Alma, "where is the Vaseline?"

Gunnar went and took the jar of Vaseline from the desk drawer, and Tinna grabbed it: "me first!"

The girls embraced the boys again, kissing them, feeling their members in their hands as they expanded, rising to their full size. Meanwhile the boys unbuttoned the girl's blouses, letting them fall, then their skirts. The girls had no underwear on beneath their school-uniforms, so once those were off the girls were nude. And they felt their boyfriend's erect penis pressing on their bare belly.

Tinna and Fleming got into bed, and Tinna began sitting beside him as he lay, and she masturbated him slowly, then she straddled him backwards, still pumping him with her hand, and let herself slide toward his face. She let go of his member as she rose to four legs, and hovered her pussy over his face, and then she lowered herself on him, his dick slipping into her mouth, her pussy on his mouth, and they lovingly pleasured each other.

Meanwhile Gunnar lay on top of Alma and they smiled as they watched them go at it.

"Do you want to do that?" asked Gunnar, his member hard between Alma's thighs.

"We can try, if we're in the mood," said Alma, pressing her thighs closer together. She could feel his erect member up against her labia, not in, but past it, his shaft in between them like an oversized hot-dog in an undersized bun, just feathering against her clit. "Can you fuck me like this?"

Gunnar moved his pelvis, grinding his shaft against her labia, pounding his thighs against her thigh, his belly against her belly, his penis stabbing his bedsheets as it emerged from between her ass-cheeks.

Alma felt happy and intimate doing this, but it wasn't working for her sexually as well as she had liked. Sure, they were naked and their genitals were touching, and he was moving on top of her, but she needed more. She needed him inside her. But not up the ass. She was about done with that. Maybe she could jerk him off, and he could lick her? That had worked before. She looked at Fleming and Tinna. Tinna was now sitting on Fleming's face, jerking him off with her hand, his hands on her hips, their bodies forming a triangle. Alma decided that she could do that. She nudged Gunnar and pointed. Gunnar nodded. He was willing to try that position. They moved around, and she placed her slit on his face and he sank his face inside her pussy and began chewing on her. It was nowhere near as pleasant as Sister Sara's oral job, that other day. Amelia found herself having difficulty holding herself balanced in this position, and fell on her face shortly after grabbing hold of Gunnar's erection. They laughed, and decided to try something else. Gunnar took the Vaseline from the table, and handed it to Alma, who smeared it liberally on his cock as they stood on their knees facing one another. When she was done, she threw the can over to Tinna and Fleming, and turned around and lay down on her belly, resting her head on her folded arms.

Gunnar began by massaging her ass, then her lower back, working his way up to her shoulders and neck, while Fleming and Tinna sat there and watched them. Then they looked at each other. It looked like a good idea to them, so they decided to massage each other as well, and they did.

Gunnar worked his way again down Alma's back, lovingly rubbing her thighs down to the knees, before he straddled her with his arms, and aimed his member in between her ass-cheeks. She was more spread now, but he still needed to work his way inside her, carefully drilling in, as she took deep, relaxing breaths.

Fleming witnessed this, and he smeared some Vaseline on his male member, and Tinna lay down flat and tried to relax as he explored her rear hole. Tinna yelped out in pain, but quickly bit on Fleming's pillow as he bored himself into her.

There was a beautiful peaceful moment as the two boys pumped the two girls in the ass in unison. They did it slowly, Alma with a serene smile on her face, pained but content, and Tinna biting down hard on the pillow, unused to the unfamiliar pain in the ass. And she thought back at the size of Gunnar's member, and wondered how Alma could stand it.

The boys came nearly simultaneously, laying flat on their girls for a few seconds to catch their breath before pulling out. Tinna ejected some feces as Fleming pulled out, and they wrapped the bedsheet up and dropped it on the floor before they lay down again to relax, post coitus. Gunnar wiped his member on a towel he found lying near by, and then he and Alma lay down, he behind her, his member between her thighs again, reaching his arms around her and stroking her clit.

They slept.

12

Alma and Tinna
streak the boys dorm

They woke up when there was a knock on the door, and the voice of Sister Rut announced: "room inspection, you have two minutes to get decent, then I'm coming in."

They had a collective shock, and jumped to their feet, all of them still naked. Fleming quickly gathered the girl's uniforms along with the soiled bedsheet, bundled the lot up and threw them out the window.

"Why'd you do that?" asked Gunnar.

"To get rid of the evidence," when Fleming noticed the nude girls there with him, he suddenly realized what he'd done, and chuckled nervously: "sorry."

Alma and Tinna wanted to scream, but that wasn't an option. The boys hurried to get on their underwear.

"Hurry, get under the bed!" Gunnar whispered at them.

"But won't the nun look under there?"

"Maybe, that's a risk we'll have to take."

Alma and Tinna got under the bed, Tinna under Fleming's, Alma under Gunnar's, and they huddled there up against the wall.

The nun opened the door and glided inside. She looked at the two boys standing there in their undies, she tried not to look at Gunnar's crotch, and she ran her eyes around the room.

"Why don't you have a bedsheet on your bed?"

"Uhm..." said Fleming, "we were trying to make a parachute from it, yesterday, uhm, and we dropped it out the window to test it."

The nun glared at him doubtfully, and she went to the window and looked outside, and saw that the bedsheet was indeed there as Fleming had said. She looked at Fleming, who made a smile at her. She shook her head: "boys," she said. She looked at the desk, and checked the drawers. She saw the Vaseline in Gunnar's bed, and glared at him, but clearly did not wish to dig deeper into it's presence there. She turned back one in the door and looked around, and at the boys, blessed them and stepped out and closed the door behind her.

They all breathed a sigh of relief, and Gunnar went and checked the nun's progress down the hall before he told the girls that it was alright to come from under the bed.

"Okay now, geniuses, when can we get dressed so we can leave here?" asked Alma.

"You can't stay here," said Fleming, "the nuns come in here while we're at breakfast and do the beds."

"What?" exclaimed Tinna, "we have to do our own beds!"

"You're girls," said Fleming.

"How can we leave then? We're naked! We'll be seen!"

"Use the bedsheet!" said Fleming, pointing at Gunnar's bedsheet.

Gunnar grabbed the bedsheet and pulled it out of his bed, and the girls wrapped themselves in it.

"Now hurry up, and try not to attract too much attention," said Gunnar, and he opened the door for the girls, and the girls stepped out, letting him close before they contemplated their next move.

Alma and Tinna were in a hallway, with many doors. It was just like the girl's dorm, with stairs down at the end, and they would then need to run the length of the next hallway to get to the stairs to the next floor down, and then repeat the process to get to the stairs down to the ground floor, where they would have to go through the dining area before they could exit through the nearest door. The building had been designed to make it quicker for the nuns to check all the rooms, not for some naked girls to get away unseen.

The girls heard a door open, and a chill ran down their back, and they ran to the stairwell. They got two steps before they found out that the bedsheet was caught in the door, and they both fell flat, buck naked on the floor.

The nude girls got up, brushing the dust off themselves, and looked at the two boys that were standing there, staring at them. The nude girls froze in their tracks and the boys were getting a great view of their exposed naked bodies as their faces grew red as tomatoes. The nude girls looked at the clothed boys, they looked so clean and tidy in their school uniforms, so wide eyed in pleasant surprise as they gazed back at the two nude girls, still standing stunned, side-by-side with their hands by their sides, their slits and breasts in full view. The nude girls turned around and made a desperate attempt to get the bedsheet for cover, pulling at it, but it was stuck firmly under the door. The boys were tilting their head at their doings, getting a great look at their jiggling asses as they struggled with the stuck cloth. They weren't far away from each other, they had a good look at them and would be able to recognize them easily, their every feature, every curve and crevice, front and back. Alma and Tinna were blushing with shame as they felt the boy's eyes on their bare asses. They gave up on the bedsheet, and decided to just make a run for it. Alma and Tinna turned around, toward the two boys, and modestly covered their slit with one hand and their breasts with the other and tiptoed past the boys, nearly touching them in the hallway, pattered down the stairwell, hands spread out for balance, and nearly ran into four boys standing around in the next hallway, just chatting. Alma and Tinna stopped and stared at them like deer in the headlights, arms up and away from their bodies. The girls recognized them; the pudgy boy they had already seen in naked, Gunnar's friend Jan, and two other boys they remembered having met in the boy's shower. Alma and Tinna were relieved to see that they had seen those boys naked, and were a little less embarrassed, they could remember them all bare as they themselves were now, and they looked at each other, biting their lips. Alma reached out for Tinna's hand, and they touched hands. The boys all looked at the nude girls as they stood there side-by-side holding hands in their most glorious natural state, breasts perky and their faces red and their exposed femininity dripping from erotic embarrassment. The boys whistled at Alma and Tinna as the nude girls smiled modestly and tiptoed past them as calmly and casually as they could, trying not to look any of them in the eye. The nude girls couldn't help smiling widely, red faced as they were. Their tingling sexual embarrassment mixed with the adrenaline rush, and they were confused about their feelings as they felt both excited and turned on, ashamed and getting moist. It was much like when they realized that the boys were watching them skinny dipping, and when Gunnar and Jan had come to their changing room dressed as nuns and seen them all. The nude girls were high on their own essences when they came down to the next floor, and didn't bother covering themselves for the boys there, waving them as they passed, addressing them for short conversation deliberately holding their hands behind their backs; walking casually, deliberately slowly past them, sometimes doubling back to pass them again, slowly turning their bodies around for display, letting the boys feast their eyes upon their feminine forms. The nude girls could feel the boys eyes warm their skin as they walked among them. The rest of the boys were down in the dining hall, laying the tables. The nude girls pirouetted for them, dancing around each of them in turn, touching them, giggling and laughing as they moved through the big room, being ogled by all the curious and pleasantly surprised boys. They both shook their tushies at them and blew them kisses before they exited, giggling as the boys cheered behind them.

The nude girls got out through the door and ran as fast as their feet would carry them back to their own dorm, the cool air wafting pleasantly across their skin. They got into the changing room, and Sister Sara didn't notice or for some other reason she did not ask them why they were already naked, or why they looked so happy.

13

Skinny dipping
with the boys

Alma met Gunnar as he was walking with his friends, Ulf, Lasse, Olof and Christian.

"Where are you going?" she asked him.

"To the lake, to swim. You want to join us?"

"I don't have a bathing suit."

"Neither do we, and from what happened yesterday, I guess neither do you."

Alma blushed. "I can't remember ever swimming in the lake in a swim suit," she admitted. They laughed. She followed them through the woods, to the lakeshore where the boys skinny dipped. The boys didn't waste any time, and got naked, throwing their clothes all around. Again she was surrounded by so many naked men at once, so many penises. All swaying when they walked. They ran around on the shore. All those penises swinging about.

There was something about almost half a dozen dangling penises coming at her that caused her to smile. The boys stood in front of her, not even thinking of covering, walked around her, encouraged her. It excited her. Then she got naked. She flung her clothes unthinkingly on the ground. Getting naked in front of the boys was so easy now. They had all seen every inch of her, she thought as she slipped her panties off and stepped out of them, she had seen all of them. And she was was alone with five boys, skinny dipping. She was nude, they were nude, penises hanging on full display for her. They didn't stay limp for long. Not when the boys had seen her naked. They surrounded her, but in a friendly way and would cock-slap her. Often in the thigh or ass, but sometimes in her face. She let them each have a go at her ass-cheeks, encouraging them to slide their members between them like hot-dogs in a bun. She got down to her knees to have them at eye level. She was such a pervy girl, she couldn't get enough of erect penis, and she tingled at the sight of those hard members and felt surges running up her spine as they slapped against her face. It didn't end there, as the boys became excited and started pumping themselves, and they lined up in front of her as she sat, legs doubled under her on the sand, watching them, blushing, anticipating. Olof was the first to cum on her face. Then Ulf and Lasse cum on her ear and her hair, respectively. She could feel the warm muck slide down to her shoulders and her chest. Christian cum just above her right eye, his semen leaking slowly into her eye, forcing her to close it. She helped Gunnar, jerking him off, opening her mouth to receive his ejaculation. It got on her nose and upper lip, and she licked it off, then licked his member. She waved the other boys to come closer, and she licked their members as well, one after the other. She looked up at Gunnar when she had Lasse's penis in her mouth, sucking it gently, and he was frowning at her. But what did he know? He was not a connoisseur of penis like she was now. When the boys had all ejaculated on Alma, they went and swam in the lake for a while, Alma to get the cum off her, the boys to get limp again. But Alma didn't like the boys to be limp, she liked them hard. She slowly emerged from the water, rinsing the water from her hair, and turned to look at them, as they swam peacefully in the lake. And she smiled erogenously, and motioned them to come out of the water. And they did. They were all still hard, except Gunnar, who was beginning to limp. She frowned, but she understood that this was an effect of having a very large member.

 "Ready for another one?" she asked.

 The boys looked at each other, and nodded. She selected Christian, and had him lie on the sand. Alma straddled him, she then asked Ulf, who like Christian had a moderately sized penis, to stick it in her ass. Ulf looked at Gunnar, who shrugged, and Ulf got down to his knees and carefully bored his member inside Alma's ass. She frowned as he entered her, but after Gunnar, this felt very comfortable to her. She clamped her thighs together on Christian's peen, and pointing Olof and Lasse to come closer and lie beside her on each side, she grabbed a hold on each of their peens with each of her hands. Finally, Gunnar eased himself in, his legs folded under him, thighs spread, and Christian moved his upper torso away, to let Alma reach her head in to suck his enormous throbbing cock.

And as Ulf began fucking Alma, she automatically ground Christian's penis between her thighs and was pushed into Gunnar's cock. Meanwhile she helped the motion by simultaneously pumping Olof and Lasse. Alma felt wild emotions run though her, as she was having as much penis as she could possibly have at the same time. In the future she would need to convince Gunnar to do this again. Not necessarily with those exact boys though, although they would now have the experience. She felt that she only needed to complete the experience with a male member actually inside her vagina, but not between her thighs. Gunnar's male member. But she had him in her mouth, and that was a comforting thought. Ulf felt rather nice in her ass, pumping her hole that had been enlarged to accommodate Gunnar, and Christian's body was so soft and nice under her. She felt Ulf come inside her, then she felt the wet slime of Christian's ejaculation about the same time as either Lasse or Olof began wetting her left hand. Gunnar then came in her mouth just before she felt the cum in her right hand.

They all lay down together, their hands gently writhing over each other's bodies as Alma un-sandwiched herself from between Ulf and Christian. Gunnar got in beside her, between her and Christian, and Ulf and Olof got between her thighs, she spread them to accommodate them, and embraced Lasse on the other side. She felt deeply desired.

The boys got dressed, and picked up her clothes for her while she washed herself in the lake again. She emerged from the lake slowly, like a Goddess, to titillate them, and then followed them through the woods in the nude, feeling like a sex Goddess, enjoying their lustful eyes upon her body.

Just as they got into view of the dormitories, the boys handed her her clothes, and she got dressed, then they said goodbye to each other and went each their own way.

14

Girl's physical examination

Since Alma was helping Sister Sara with the measurements, she got to have her measurements taken first, in private. Which meant that she got to take a bath in Sara's chamber. Alma wished she could have a bathtub in her room. She would have sacrificed Tinna's bed for it, and just slept on top of Tinna the whole time.

The bath was warm, and Sister Sara allowed Alma to stay submerged in it, to relax for an hour, while Sara herself sat at her little desk and prepared the measurement documents. She wore her glasses to see the documents, elegant black rimmed glasses, that made her look sexy. The warm water embraced Alma's entire body, so gently and so intimately. She had her hair tied up in a bun, so as not to get it wet. There was no reason for her to do the girl's measurements while looking like a dog. She washed herself in no hurry, slowly lathering her arms, then her legs, one at a time, when she felt like moving. She carefully washed her vagina underwater, and while she was rubbing her own labia clean, she thought that she might just finish herself while she was at it, flicking herself off while her hands and her pussy were invisible from the surface. She gently rubbed her clit, making small, circular motions, not stirring up the water too much so as not to alert Sister Sara of her sinful behavior. She bit her lip. She had not felt this comfortable at the school, ever.

"Oh, you sinful girl."

Alma was shocked out of her reverie by Sister Sara, who stood over her, looking down on her with a wicked smile, slowly shaking her head. She had removed her glasses.

"Ah... sorry..."

"You must do fifty hail Mary's for that," said Sister Sara.

Alma had cold sweat running all over her, despite being in the warm tub.

"But don't worry now. Now finish cleaning yourself and get out from the tub. I'll dry you."

Alma rose to her feet, and let the water run from her smooth skin for a moment before she stepped out of the tub, and Sister Sara helped dry her body with a towel. She did it with an easy smile, which made Alma feel weird. She finally hung up the towel, and came to Alma, standing much too close to her, and said to her, gently stroking her arms: "have you been feeling lonely? All alone here surrounded by just those teenage girls and no physical contact?"

Alma felt better knowing that Sister Sara didn't seem to suspect anything about her or the other girl's escapades. And she didn't feel like letting her know, that would have to stay a secret for longer, she preferred forever. She looked back into Sara's myopic eyes and nodded.

Sister Sara embraced her, firmly but gently. To Alma's alarm, she then kissed her on the cheek, and again, closer to her mouth, and then on her lips, in such a loving way. Alma was wide eyed, but Sister Sara had her eyes closed, and she was kissing Alma so sensuously, and she felt Sara's hands slowly run down her back, stroking her bum, grasping her ass-cheeks as she licked Alma's lips. Sister Sara loosened her grasp and pulled away from Alma, looking at Alma's nude body with her bedroom eyes; she looked from her knees to her luscious pussy, from her mons up along her flat belly, at her perky breasts, up her neck and into her sweet eyes, and she turned around and made Alma sit on the bed. Alma could see where this was going. She swallowed hard, and allowed Sister Sara to spread her legs. She was going to do that thing again.

Sister Sara was very good at licking pussy. She made practiced motions with her tongue, knew where to bite, where and when to kiss, what to suck. Alma's eyes rolled all the way back in her head so that she could see the inside of her skull. Gunnar was not this good. Having Gunnar for a husband and sleeping with him was great, but in the future she contemplated getting Sister Sara for a visit to give her cunnilingus. Or at the very last have her teach Gunnar how.

Alma quaked with ecstasy and squirted in Sister Sara's face. Sister Sara wiped her face with the bedclothes, and crawled into bed with Alma fully clothed, laying down beside her, stroking her bare belly, rubbing her face against Alma's cheek.

"We still have time, do you want to do me?" she asked Alma.

Alma thought about it. It sounded disgusting, but she wished to keep Sister Sara on her side in case she discovered her doing anything worse than just masturbating in her tub. So she nodded. Sister Sara smiled. It was such a bright and happy smile. Sara rose up.

"You don't have to take it all off," said Alma, and Sister Sara paused. She smiled, and carefully slid down her undies. Alma looked at Sara's undies, and thought that it was one of the drawbacks to being a nun, not having access to sexy underwear.

Sister Sara sat on the edge of the bed, and Alma slid out of bed and crawled in between her thighs. Alma lifted Sara's skirt, and moved in, under her skirt. She saw Sister Sara's pussy, it was clean and smelled faintly of soap. It occurred to Alma that she was the second person to use that bath-water. She moved in closer, first blowing softly on Sara's pussy, then licking her gently. Alma had little practice in this, so she approached this like she was French kissing someone sideways. She licked Sara's soft and thick vaginal lips and bit her roast-beef, furtively tasting her. She tasted better than Alma had expected, almost pleasant. It felt warm and nice under the skirt, and if not for the feeling of disgust at having to lick another woman, if would have been the nicest, most intimate feeling. Alma thought as she licked Sara's slit like an ice-cream, that she was so happy that Sara hadn't disrobed. Licking the pussy of a naked woman would have made her feel like she was engaging in some lesbian sex act. She sucked on Sara's clit, sticking her tongue in her and mouthing it with her lips and her teeth. Sister Sara started quaking, he pussy vibrating against Alma's mouth. Suddenly Sara's feminine essences welled up and forcefully entered Alma's mouth and ran down her cheeks and chin. Sara moaned, almost like a cat meowing.

Alma backed out from under her skirt, and stood up and reached for the towel.

"Thank you," said Sister Sara. She stood up, and when Alma had dried her juice from her face, she took her by the forearm and said: "now let's measure you."

Sister Sara dragged Alma out of her chamber, completely nude, and all the way to the nurses room, which was on the second floor. The air in the hallways on the way was cool, and felt even cooler as Alma was slightly wet from sweat, after her stay under Sister Sara's skirt. They met a few nuns in the way, and a couple of girls. The nuns didn't look at her and Alma didn't react to them, and only the girls saw reason to look after her as she passed. They had seen each other nude before, just not in the hallways like that, but it was still a little embarrassing to her. Strangely, Alma felt almost as embarrassed as when she had streaked the boys dormitory. On the way Alma got a slight kick out of knowing that Sister Sara wasn't wearing any underpants.

The nurse was a middle aged friendly woman, getting gray haired, dressed like Sister Sara. But she was probably wearing her undies. Alma didn't want to ask. The nurse was in no way bothered by Alma's nudity, and she asked Alma some questions, then measured her height, her chest, her waist and her hips, noting it all down. She then had Alma step on some scales, and fiddled with them to tell Alma to the gram how much she weighed. Then she smiled and told Alma that she was normal and average in every way, and looked healthy.

Alma followed Sister Sara to Alma's dorm room, where she finally got dressed. The physical exam was held in the school gymnasium. It was partitioned off, and the girls were taken in three at a time, where the school nurse would ask one some questions while one was being measured and another being weighed, all in the nude. Alma and Sara walked in where all the girls stood waiting in two lines, each wrapped in a towel, entering their little partitioned examining area. One of the Sisters, Sister Maria, then led the girls to the little partitioned off room, Sister Rut taking their towel before they entered in the nude. Sara oversaw the scales, while Alma and Sister Fransesca helped measuring the girls, Alma measuring, while Fransesca noted it down. They had some extra measurements, like the width of their thigh gap, and recording whether they had an innie or an outie pussy, and the shape of their breasts. Alma was sure that this was for sake of Sara's personal perversions, and she just shook her head and shrugged. None of the girls were bothered by any of this, as they were used to Sister Sara's much more invasive daily routine in the shower. They just smiled at Alma and giggled a little when she touched their privates. Alma blushed.

Once the girls had been measured, they walked out of the partitioned room, and got to walk naked through a long partitioned off hallway to where they had left their clothes in charge of two nuns.

15

Boy's physical examination

The boy's physical exam was held the next day. Alma and Tinna met with the other girls who were there to help instead of the nuns; Anna, Liv and Thalia. Just Sister Sara and Sister Rut were there on behalf of the nuns. Girls named Becky and Ingrid agreed to guard the clothes.

They boys were already undressed when the nuns arrived with all the girls, all lined up in two rows like the girls before them, each with his own modesty towel rapped around his waist. There were only 25 boys in the school, so this would take less time than with the girls. The girls blushed slightly when they walked past the bare-chested boys in their towels on their way to the examination room, and their anticipation grew. The boys were blushing too, and some looked uneasy. Most of them recognized Alma and Tinna from before, and smiled at them.

Alma and Tinna knew why they were smiling, and blushed even more. Alma gave Gunnar a luscious smile when she passed him.

The girls entered the partitioned off examination area, and greeted the school nurse. Then they could begin. Sister Sara led in the first three boys, and Sister Rut took their towels and turned away, and the nude boys covered their genitals with their hands and walked in, uneasily looking around, smiling at the fully clothed girls, and the girls blushed and smiled back.

Anna's job was to guide the naked boys to the right place, and she began taking the first one by the arm and leading him to talk to the nurse, then she led the next one to Alma and Tinna, who did the measurements, and the third to Liv and Thalia, who were operating the scales.

The naked boys could cover their peen as they were being weighed, despite Liv and Thalia's best efforts to move their hands away, but they had to hold their arms apart while Tinna measured their chest and waist and Alma crouched down and measured their hips.

Alma paused for a moment, as Tinna lifted the

naked boy's arms, and she had his peen right in front of her face. It was limp, slightly offset to the side, veiny, dangling from it's furry nest, it's tip reaching below the balls. Much larger than that statue of David had promised, as she could remember from her trip to the boy's showers and that time she spied on the boys as the were skinny dipping, and as she had joined them... But not as big as Gunnar's. Despite her experience she felt her face heat up. She measured it, and found it to be 11 cm long, limp. She reached around the boy's waist, and measured his hips. She saw that his member rose and expanded as she measured, and she touched it, feeling it's softness, and it grew more, and she kissed it and it jerked up. She measured it again, and found it to have become 14 cm long. She called out the numbers, and Thalia wrote them down. She let him go, and received the next boy, who already had a substantial erection, but she only found it to be 13 cm long. She touched it some, just to see it jerk up, and played with its foreskin, folding it up away from his tip a little, trying to look professional. Tinna stood next to the boy and waited while she did this, and they smiled at each other. Alma held the boy's peen in her hand and gave him a soft jerk before she let him go.

Anna stood by the exit and insisted on kissing every boy who left, grabbing some of them in the ass, feeling of them in the scrotum, or running her fingers along their hard, erect shaft, or just giving them a hug, feeling their erection against her lower abdomen. She was all smiles.

Alma was exposed to all the penises, and some of them touched her face as she reached around the boy's waist to measure their hips, especially when they were erect, which was always when they came to her after being interviewed and weighed first. Alma had to also measure the length and girth of their penis, which she had to do quickly, since they tended to expand and rise as she fondled them. She was supposed to get two measurements, limp, and erect. She got much more measurements of them erect. Only one boy managed to be limp for the whole procedure.

Liv and Thalia were very touchy and feely with the rest of the naked boys, and always sent them fully erect to Alma and Tinna. Liv and Thalia would try to jerk the boy's hands away, to sneak a peek at them, and then "accidentally" touch them. Alma saw them both on several occasions holding a boy's member in their hand for more than just a few seconds. Often while the other held his hands away.

The school nurse quickly became red faced when she had to interview the naked boys with their full erection. Some of them became erect so quickly that Alma could not get a limp measurement, and she ended up only recording 5. She and the other girls were happy to see the pudgy boy, who Liv had sucked in the forest some days before. His member was so cute and tiny, just 7 cm long when erect. Alma sneaked to kiss it. So did both Liv and Thalia, making up excuses to lean down and kiss him, and lick him. They had their hands all over him. He was such a cute boy, and they all wanted to try out his cute little member, it would fit inside their mouth, it wouldn't hurt in their ass, it was so fun to touch and fondle. He came to Alma after his weighing, already very excited, and Tinna just had to reach around him while Alma was measuring his hips, and he came on her face. His cum hit her right above her left eye. Alma frowned at first, but then she could but giggle at the event. Tinna giggled so much. The boy looked sheepish.

Alma could satisfy her curiosity about the true size of Gunnar's member. It was 22 cm long, and it took her full two minutes to get it to rise to it's fullest extent to get that measurement. He cock-slapped her twice while she was trying to get more rise out of him, once on each cheek. Alma giggled, but caught his dick in her hands again and jerked him until he was no longer soft and floppy. He nearly came. Alma was his last stop, so he did not need to make the nurse any redder than she was by showing his erection to her.

The naked boys did not cover themselves in any way as they returned to where Becky and Ingrid stood guard over their clothes, and Becky and Ingrid got to see them come at them fully erect, their members all bobbing and wobbling as they walked. Becky and Ingrid also gave the boys a kiss and a hug, and their boyfriends waited with them after they arrived, and watched the other boys receive their clothes and leave holding them, to stroll naked to their dormitories. The boyfriends waited, just standing there with them in the nude, until they were alone with their Becky and Ingrid, and then the boys received a blow-job from them.

Becky and Ingrid were still sucking their boyfriends when Alma, Tinna, Anna and the rest came, and saw them. The boys waved at them when they saw them come walking.

"You have to finish quickly, before Sister Sara or Rut sees you," said Alma.

The boys nodded, smiling as Becky and Ingrid sucked them.

"I'll go and stall them," said Anna with a smile, and jogged back.

The boys gave her a thumbs up. The girls stood around and watched as Becky and Ingrid finished their boyfriends, Alma a little jealous of them at being able to so easily give their boyfriends head. Afterwards, Becky and Ingrid licked them clean, wiped their lips, and stood up as the boys picked up their bundle of clothes, and covering their privates with them, walked out of the gymnasium in the nude, and went to their dorm.

16

Sister Sara watches Alma and Gunnar have sex

Sister Sara and two of the nuns saw the boys come out of the gymnasium naked and unconcerned, holding their clothes. They crossed themselves, but watched them pass. The boys nodded toward them. Sister Sara frowned. She had seen them well, as she was wearing her glasses at that moment. They also saw the girls leave, with wide smiles on their red faces. Sister Sara raised an eyebrow. She walked into the gymnasium and talked to the school nurse, who gave her a detailed report. Sister Sara listened, and tried not to show emotion when she heard about how Alma had taken some extra time to masturbate one of the boys, Gunnar, the one with the largest penis. He had let her play with his dick, unembarrassed as he stood nude in front of her, and they had looked very happy and playful.

Sister Sara decided to follow Alma. So she put on her glasses and followed her around from a safe distance. She didn't need to follow her for long, for after dinner she disappeared into the nearby woods, where Gunnar was waiting for her. Sister Sara sneaked after them deeper into the woods. She could hear that they were deep in conversation, but she was too far away to hear what they were saying.

Suddenly they stopped, and Gunnar pushed Alma up against a tree. Sister Sara hid behind another tree, her heart racing in her bosom. She looked slowly from behind the tree, and saw that Gunnar was kissing Alma. He had his arms around her, and they were sharing a passionate kiss. Sara frowned. She'd never experienced that, and upon thinking about it, guessed it would be unlikely. She being a nun, and all that... she envied Alma so much. She continued watching. Gunnar and Alma kissed for a long time, their hands roaming wildly up and down each other's body as they writhed up against that tree. She could see Alma's hands reach down to Gunnar's zipper, and undoing it, and Sara saw

Alma's hand disappear into his pants, and start moving about in a sort of a pumping motion. She took her hand out, and used both hands to undo his belt, and they both turned around, and this time Alma held Gunnar up against the tree-trunk. His pants fell down, and she looked him in the eye, seductively biting her lower lip, before she lowered herself to her knees. Sister Sara saw Alma reach up and drag Gunnar's underpants down, revealing his large, erect penis. Sister Sara drooled. She was getting moist. She watched Alma lick the tip of Gunnar's penis, and it throbbed in her hands as she did. She opened her mouth and took it in, as much as would fit, and mouthfucked him. As she mouthfucked him, she lifted her skirt up and reached in under her panties with one hand and touched herself.

Sister Sara was breathing heavily as she watched Alma pump Gunnar's dick in her mouth and twirl her hand on herself, as she slowly dragged up her long black nun-skirt, and reached into her large, comfortable, figure hugging nun-undies, and her fingers found her own nun-slit. It was a secret that she did this every time after she'd touched the girls in the shower-room, but she'd never done it out in the woods before. Her fingers knew her clit well and she believed that it was tainted with the essence of every girl's slit she'd ever touched. Hundreds of them. She liked to think of her pussy as having experienced the ghost of all the girl's slits, she had dreamt of it, the ghost of the Holy Vagina, it was slick and wet and untouched by penis.

When Alma had received Gunnar's splooge, she licked his dick clean, and then she rose up and they hugged again, and started kissing. Sister Sara saw Gunnar spit on the ground shortly after, as Alma giggled. Then she reached under her skirt and pulled off her panties. She turned and walked a few steps, then turned again, and sat down, then lay back, propped up on her arms.

Sister Sara was feeling nice and warm, with pleasant streams coming in pulses from her slida as she reached her fingers as deep inside herself as they would go. Her glasses were fogging up and she was leaking feminine fluid in her panties, and would need to address that when she returned, before the other nuns could smell her. Meanwhile, Gunnar stepped out of his pants, and got down on his knees and then lay down and went between Alma's thighs, holding them apart by the knees as he leaned down toward her belly. Alma pulled up her skirt and lifted her ass off the ground to get her pussy closer to his face, and he leaned in and started licking her. Alma made a face as if she were moaning, but silently, and Sister Sara felt it sympathetically as she herself rubbed her G-spot.

Alma yelped softly like a puppy when she came. Sister Sara was by now leaning with one hand up against the tree, while gently fondling her own intricate labia, now going at it harder and faster than before, all the while keeping an eye on those two good, sexy students. Sara felt a surge of erotic energy when she witnessed Gunnar rise to his knees, his penis firm and directed at Alma, while Alma rolled on to her belly, and rose to all fours. And Sister Sara watched, cotton-brained with sexual pleasure as Gunnar bored his dick into Alma's ass.

"So that's how they do it without me finding

out about it," said Sara to herself. She was too sexed to feel angry. But now she wanted some of that dick.   After that, those girls could fuck whoever they wanted. Yes, from now on, she'd have their boyfriends. While they watched.

Sister Sara's eyes rolled as her slida released a spray of feminine juices into her hand, her undies, her thighs. Her whole body convulsed, vibrated in satisfaction and she became limp as a sponge, she could see stars. She breathed deep a few times and relaxed.   Gunnar was still fucking Alma in the ass, and their whole attention was on that, while Sara slowly stood to her feet and let herself slide back into the woods, leaving for her chamber to plot her next move.

17

All the boys get naked for the girls

Alma and Tinna walked into the boys changing room after their football practice; Alma to meet Gunnar, Tinna to see Fleming, both of them to see the boys naked. Some of the boys were naked already when the girls entered their changing room, and the boys were a little bit startled to see Alma and Tinna in their dressing room as they stood there with their bodies exposed, genitals hanging limp for the girls to see, but the boys greeted Alma and Tinna well this time because they knew the two girls, they had seen both Alma and Tinna in all their bare-assed glory, and they were also well desensitized to being naked with the girls. So the boys just continued undressing or standing around naked as Alma and Tinna walked past them on their way to the shower. The naked boys in the shower cheered the girls when they saw them, and invited them into the shower room. Alma and Tinna accepted their invitation, and walked in there fully dressed and found themselves surrounded by 10 naked and wet and well built boys. The boys looked at ease and smiling, letting it all hang, and Alma and Tinna blushed a little, seeing all those penises, though they had seen them all before, but naked men are naked men to a girl, and so many penises are still erotic in their way. Alma and Tinna cast their glance at the hanging penises, comparing them, admiring them, touching some of them, fantasizing about the smaller penises, since taking it up the ass was always painful though they were slowly getting used to it. And there stood Gunnar, with the biggest penis, already slowly filling with blood, and he smiled at Alma. Tinna found Fleming, and she hugged him and gave him a kiss under the shower's warm stream as the other boys watched with envy in their eyes while blood flowed to their dicks.

Some other girls saw as Alma and Tinna and filed in after them, and that led to girls calling out to each other that they were all meeting in the boy's dressing room. The boys had undressed completely and were all bare ass-naked before half of the girls had entered the dressing room. Some of the boys were a bit red faced, but they didn't cover, and the girls squeaked with glee, looking at the naked boys, sensuously eyeing their exposed dicks, biting their lips, getting a little moist. In time, all the girls had enthusiastically entered the boy's dressing room.

The nuns noticed this movement of the girls pouring into the boys dressing room, and one went and informed Sister Sara while two of them entered the dressing room to serve as chaperones. The nuns were disturbed to see all those nude boys, all those exposed penises, penises that were in all cases erect and in many cases being fondled by the girls, in one case even being sucked. Sister Sara was close by, and when she went in to the boys dressing room, she found the lecherous boys all naked and fully erect by the horny girls who were still all wearing their formal skirt and cotton blouse, many were paired up, some boys had two girls. The atmosphere was charged with sexuality.

Sara went and looked into the shower, and found 10 couples standing there, hugging and kissing, each under their own shower, the girls still wearing their now drenched uniforms while their male partners were all fully nude and erect.

"Stop this this instant!" called Sister Sara loudly into the shower.

The couples looked at her, and were visibly startled, immediately stopping their sexual writhing and placed themselves side by side.

Sister Sara felt a tingle of erotic sensuality in her slida as she beheld all those erect penises directed at her. She breathed through her teeth. She thought about starting doing a morning shower routine on the boys. She might line them all up and stroke them and have them all rise... No, she had to be with the girls, they were pure, they were soft and beautiful. She walked into the shower room, in between the amorous couples, toward Alma and Gunnar. Alma was still holding on to Gunnar with both arms. Gunnar was facing Sara, his large erect penis pointing defiantly at her. She stood and looked at him for a few seconds, impressed by his size.

"There you are, you two," she finally said.

Gunnar and Alma looked at each other, clearly confused, then at Sister Sara.

"I know about you," said Sara, menacingly, looking them each in the eye. She glanced down at Gunnar's large penis again, then she said: "all of you get out."

Sister Sara walked out of the shower: "everybody out! Now! Don't bother dressing, you clearly don't care for that. Follow me out into the school grounds."

All the students followed after Sister Sara, the boys all completely naked as they were, and the girls all dressed, though some of them would have preferred to remove their wet clothes, followed then by the nuns.

The sun was shining and the weather was pleasant, with a little wind blowing softly, rustling the leaves and the grass as they exited the building. On the school grounds, Sister Sara had them all line up facing each other, boys on one side, wet and naked, none of them bothering to cover themselves, proud of their hard-on, girls on the other, dressed, watching the boys intently, leeringly, erogeneously, and she spoke to them: "you disgusting perverts! What are you thinking to be engaging in impure actions like I just witnessed now, in school? I will punish you all for this. The one's responsible I will punish more. Now who instigated this mess?"

The students looked around at each other, and grinned.

"Confess! Confess, you who began this indecency, and I'll be lenient with the rest of you."

Alma raised her hand.

"You! Explain your actions!"

"I was just visiting my boyfriend in the shower, and I don't know why, but all the other girls just followed me..."

"I'll deal with them later," she turned to the boys: "I will have you go naked for a week, since you enjoyed it so much!"

The girls giggled and the boys all grinned, their already hard cocks throbbing a little at the words. Sister Sara saw that, and re-considered: "you're enjoying this, aren't you? You perverts!"

Sister Sara was angry, and she took a few deep breaths to calm herself down and took time to think up a good punishment, one that would actually be punishing. She looked at the line of formally dressed girls and the opposite line of bare-naked boys, all with their throbbing erections, and she watched how they all looked each other up, leering lasciviously at each other, clearly enjoying the situation. She spotted Gunnar's large cock, and looked him up and in the eye, the heat of her carnal desire fogging her lenses; the next few were normal, looking small in comparison until she came upon the chubby boy, with his little finger-sized dick, small, but erect and throbbing, and she thought: "what a tiny penis," and found herself wondering if it would feel good entering her ass? Sara imagined how the school would be if she had all those boys walk around naked, with their constant throbbing late teen-erections around all those obviously madly horny girls, only needing to hide behind a corner and slip down a panty and insert themselves to get off. She thought about smacking their penises with a ruler. The thought made her great pleasure, and she decided she'd have to do that to one or two or three of them some day. It would have to be painful and embarrassing for all of them. She looked at the array of throbbing erect penises, and had an idea.

"You!" she pointed at the girls: "take off your clothes!"

The girls stopped giggling and looked at her with a confused expression.

"All of them! Now!"

"But the boys..." said one of the girls, who was cut off by Sister Sara: "take them all off. Take your clothes off right now this instant and lay them on the ground."

The girls shot worried glances at each other, then at Sister Sara, meeting her angry glare, and began reluctantly undressing. Alma and Tinna got undressed just after Anna and Liv, who were happy to get naked, boys or no boys, followed by the others in short order, with Maria and Samantha getting naked last, and those two stood coyly covering themselves, slit and breast with their hands. Half the girls saw need to cover either their slit or their breasts, the rest had been in the woods or been skinny dipping with the boys in their free time so they saw no reason to.

With all those heavenly bodies bare before them, not a stitch to defile their beauty, the boys became even harder, their breath labored, their faces more expectant. They looked uneasy, horny and ready to jump into action at the array of slick, ready female bodies in front of them, to grab those varied soft breast, hold those wide, sensuous hips, thrust their dicks into those virgin slits, grind their own hard abs against the girl's soft flat abs, warp their legs together and kiss those luscious lips while fucking hard and fast. With that line of sexy nude girls to choose from, it would be only a question of which one they caught hold of first.

Sister Sara gave them all a time to get a good look at each other's nudity, take it all in, get a bit hot, before she announced: "now you boys, you go and put on their clothes."

The boys looked at each other, confused, then at the girl's uniforms on the ground in front of the nude girls. The nude girls were frowning, not liking this new development.

"Put them on. Pick one that is close to your size and wear it. I mean all of it. The bra as well. Go on."

The boys reluctantly walked to the clothes, and looking the girls up for size comparison, not for sexual pleasure, they selected the uniform they thought might fit them the best, and started getting dressed.

The girls forgot their embarrassment at being naked and started giggling as the boys put on their clothes, they looked so weird. When they were all wearing the girls uniform, Sister Sara said: "now this is what you will be wearing for the rest of the school year. The girls will be naked. NAKED! And the boys will wear girls clothes. And makeup. And if they don't, I'll hit them in the ball-sack with my ruler. In front of everybody!"

The boys looked very confused, not all of them seemed to mind too much, but for most this sounded like bad news. The girls stopped giggling and looked worried.

Sister Sara pointed Alma and Gunnar to come with her. They followed her.

17

Sister Sara
and Alma and Gunnar
have a threesome

Alma and Gunnar anxiously followed Sister Sara to Sara's chamber. Sister Sara was in no hurry as she pointed the pair to enter the chambers before her, which they quietly did, and she silently wafted in after them, carefully closing the door, and she locked it and took the key and pocketed it. There she stood, leaning against the door, and she looked at the two of them, as they stood there, facing her; Alma still naked, now modestly covering her breasts and her slit, and Gunnar, wearing Anna's school-uniform but holding the panties in his right hand, looking foolish, his half-erection obvious under the skirt.

Sara peered as she looked the two of them up and down, with a hint of an angry glare. The walk up the stairs to her chambers had calmed her a little bit, but she was still steaming with carnal lust.

"Hands by your sides!" Sister Sara commanded, and Alma moved her hands from her breasts and her slit and stood fully exposed to Sara's glare.

Sara looked Alma up again, slowly taking in her body, her soft, luscious pussy with its delectable clit between the softly furry labia, Sara wanted to run her fingers through that tuft of hair, between those soft labia and lick that delicious soft clit. She took a deep breath. That girl needed to be punished. Sister Sara looked at where Gunnar's erection rose under his newly acquired skirt, and ran her tongue around her lips. She addressed him: "did the girls get you off?"

"Excuse me?"

"When you were in the yard having your penis licked by the girls, did you come? Did you ejaculate? Did splooge issue from your penis?"

"Eh... no."

Sister Sara smiled. "Take off that silly outfit," she ordered him.

Gunnar and Alma looked at each other.

"Take it off."

Gunnar dropped the panties on the floor, and began taking off the girl's blouse. He had the bra underneath, but he'd not been able to fasten it in the back, so he got it off with ease. He dropped the skirt, and his large, throbbing erection bounced a little. Alma covered her blushing smile with her hand. Sister Sara smiled. She began taking off her nun-attire, slwoly, in front of the two of them. One after another, articles of nun-attire slipped to the floor, until Sister Sara stood there naked before them, wearing a malicious smile.

"I know you two have been fucking in the woods. I have seen you. I also know that you haven't been penetrated vaginally," she said this, looking them in the eyes, from one to the other and back, always wearing the same malicious smile, "that's why I am going to fuck your boyfriend. My vagina will be the first vagina he enters, not yours, mine."

Sister Sara stepped toward Gunnar, and grabbed him by the shaft of his firmly erect penis, and pulled him, softly but firmly toward her. She put his penis between her thighs and made full body contact with him, from her mons venus to her small, flat breasts, holding him tight: "you will fuck me, then I'll maybe let you fuck her." And she kissed him full on the mouth, a wet, sensuous, passionate kiss before she pushed him on the bed. Gunnar bounced on the spring bed, and Sister Sara got in bed after him and moved over him, straddling him, and Alma saw as she lowered herself on top of him, guiding his penis into her vagina, and she watched in silence as Gunnar's penis sank inside Sister Sara's slida, all the way. She could see as it displaced her flesh, it's shape printing visibly on her Mons Venus. Sister Sara felt that Gunnars penis was wider and longer than she had expected, his girth filled her slida firmly and painfully but so pleasurably, and the penis was also longer than the vagina, and pushed though the cervix and touched the fundus.

Alma saw the pain in Sara's expression as she self-impaled on Gunnar's dick, and worried about her future as recipient of that same penis. But all she could do was to look on with envy as Sister Sara rode her boyfriend, pain be damned.

Alma watched with hypnotic awe as Gunnar's thick, oily wet shaft pumped in and out of Sara's tight slit, visible on her lower abdomen, that was so gross, yet so erotic and she found herself moisten. Alma knew full well how tight and petite and inexperienced in penile reception Sister Sara's pussy was, after all, she had licked her, and she felt sympathetic pains with Sara as she fucked her boyfriend. The pain and regret in Sara's expression slowly subsided though, and she began looking triumphantly at Alma, who stood by and quietly ran her fingers through her slit as she watched them.

Sister Sara pulled up Gunnars hands, and had him fondle her little breasts. He obliged, and Alma frowned, after all, he was her boyfriend, her was supposed to do that to her.

Sister Sara stopped fucking Gunnar, sitting on him, his penis resting firm against her fundus, and Sara pointed Alma to get in bed. Alma complied, and Sara leaned over, laying down on Gunnar, and they rolled over, Gunnar on top of Sara.

"Now, you sit on my face, and you two kiss while he fucks me," she said, pointing Alma to come and sit on her face.

That sounded good to Alma, as she knew that Sara was a master pussy-licker, pleaser of schoolgirls, and they all got into position: Sara on her back, her legs spread wide to accommodate Gunnar's thrusts, and Alma spreading her pussy over Sara's face for her to lick. Meanwhile Gunnar and Alma leaned into one another and held their hands on each other's shoulder while they kissed, and Gunnar pushed his dick deep into Sara from his foothold on the floorboard.

Gunnar fucked Sara slowly, while he passionately kissed Alma, who kissed back with enthusiastic romance while Sara lovingly licked her clit. Alma felt more accepted than before, and she was beginning to like Sara, despite her rape of her boyfriend. She was being physically romanced at both ends, and it was such a lovely feeling. She knew that they would all have to get together and do this again.

Alma was seeing stars when she squirted her pussy juice all over Sara's face, and she realized that Gunnar offloaded his splooge inside Sara at the same moment.

Afterwards, they lay both by Sara's side, stroking her body lovingly, softly, fingers making adventures into her feminine crevice. Sara didn't mind. She didn't even mind when Gunnar rolled over her, and on top of Alma, who received him in her loving arms. She bit her lip and watched as Gunnar's penis sank into Alma's slit. Alma felt as his tip, wet and slippery with Sara's pussy-juice, parted her labia, and slid into her slida, filling her vagina, she felt his tip slide inside her, through her hymen, touching every square centimetre of the inside of her vagina, she felt it come in contact with her cervix. It was the most loving intimate feeling she'd ever experienced. And then he started fucking her, first gently, then harder, as Sister Sara lay beside them and watched their bodies undulate together, her fingers in her own slit, slowly churning her clit. She came, moaning softly, and fell asleep, rocked into the dreamland by Alma and Gunnar's motions, and when Gunnar and Alma noticed, they smiled and continued fucking until they came, and then they got out of bed.

"She is cute when she sleeps," said Gunnar,

watching Sister Sara naked in bed.

"Don't get any ideas."

18

Punishment

Lasse and the pudgy boy stood by the showers, wearing their girls-uniforms as they handed the towels to the girls as they emerged naked and wet from the showers. The girls had given up on modesty, there was no longer any point in covering their privates, so they didn't. The boys were red faced, but looked happy, if discomforted by their raging erections that they wee too busy to adjust properly in their tight fitting girl's panties. The girls smiled at them when they received their towels and dried themselves, making a huge show out of it for them. All those unrelenting bouncing breasts and bare pussies and jiggling asses kept the boys uncomfortably firm, and the girls knew it, and Sister Sara had promised to kick them in the groin if they removed their uncomfortably tight panties.

Sister Sara had the door to the girl's dressing room removed, and the boys were encouraged to enter and watch the girls shower, which they did, all of them, except Gunnar, Alma looked around for him but didn't see him, and the boys were sitting, most of them, on the benches where the girl's clothes would normally be and stared, red faced and wide eyed at the girls as they entered the showers in batches, while most of the girls stood outside and waited, bare assed for the boys to behold. Some of the girls glared at them, still not over their humiliation, most of them just giggled and enjoyed themselves. They felt better being naked together, at least they were sharing the experience. After yesterday, none of them covered themselves, embarrassed or not. The boys had already seen it all, their most intimate parts, but that wasn't to say they were getting bored of seeing their intimate parts. Some of the boys stood around and talked to the nude girls, it all looked like easy conversation too. Sister Sara, Alma and Tinna and Anna walked around the room and made sure that any boy and girl stayed a meter apart, should they converse with one another. Sister Sara did that in a harsh tone, but Alma and the girls did it in a sensuous tone and with a smile, and most couples complied without being asked, the boys only too happy to be able to view their girlfriend's bodies more fully.

The proper embarrassment began when Sister Sara had all the naked girls line up, and she and Alma went from one to another, Sara followed by Lasse and Alma by the pudgy boy, and did their morning routine on the girls while the boys watched in amazed glee. The girls, apart from Anna, Liv and two or three others were so embarrassed they could have died, while many of the boys had premature ejaculations in their panties. Alma was half way through her line, and she frowned as she saw the pudgy boy shake a bit, making his little O face, and knew that he'd just ejaculated beside her. He'd cum, right in his panties, just from being surrounded by all thsoe nude young girls. White slime would be pumping out of his dick, right into the fabric of the panties, drenching it. He made her a little guilty glance, but seemed calmer and more adjusted afterwards.

Sister Sara made Alma, Tinna, Anna, Liv and a

sensual curvy blonde named Diana wait after the shower. They waited until the last of the girls had left, happy and dry and freshly fingered, their ample bare asses jiggling like jell-o as they tiptoed out through he doorway, and then the boys filed out after them, their still raging boners causing them to walk strangely as their cum hardened in their panties.

"I have decided your punishment," Sister Sara began, and the girls looked at each other.

"But I thought that being naked for the rest of the school-year was the punishment?" asked Diana before Alma could ask that same question. She even had the same words all lined up in her mind.

"You all know that's not punishment enough," said Sister Sara, taking two steps and she eyed the five of them as they stood naked before her, already getting used to their daily routine of being fingered by her and Alma.

Sara looked Diana in the eye: "you five will teach the boys to do the morning examination. Then, after that, the boys will be doing the morning pussy examination on you... while I watch, of course."

The girls looked at each other, in openmouthed surprize. Anna and Liv looked at each other, biting their lips.

"They will be more thorough. They will be taste testing your slits directly, three of them, to be sure. Those who's pussies don't taste clean will be sponge bathed," said Sara, looking at Diana, from her thin thighs with her wide pussy gap, with her protruding inner labia, up her flat stomach along her whole lithe shape to her perky little breasts, thin neck, surprizingly round face with her blue eyes and strong, perky cheeks and kissable lips.

Anna and Liv looked excited. Alma and Tinna tried to not look like they looked forward to it, while Diana looked as passive as ever.

"I had the nuns gather the boys, they will be waiting outside on the football field for you to teach them. If you don't, they'll know little when I have them examine you tomorrow, so teach them well."

***

As Sister Sara had told them, the boys were on

the football field, all 25 of them, looking rather silly in their girl's uniforms; the pleated skirts and cotton blouses. The girls saw them as they finished adjusting their penises in their panties, and wiped the cum off their hands in their skirts. It was disgusting.

Tinna said to Alma as they walked to the boys: "I'd be so mortified if this happened on my first day."

Alma looked at her.

"Imagine having to be naked in front of all the boys on the first day."

"We're naked now."

"It's not the same. We were naked yesterday too, and we have kind of exposed ourselves before, and we've both had dick inside us. It's different for us now, we're used to it."

"I already had sex before I came here," said Diana.

The girls looked at her.

"I have a boyfriend, or had. I don't know now. Sister Sara knew, so she wasn't upset when she fingered me. She always fingers me deep, like she appreciates it. Then she always rubs my labia." Diana had an outie, like Sara, that Alma thought looked disgusting, but was all soft and pliable and she liked touching it too.

Alma decided not to tell Diana about Sister Sara. She was sure that she could smell the odor of cum wafting off the boys as they came nearer, and the boys watched them arrive. They were all there, regardless of wether they knew how to touch a girl or not, even Gunnar. Gunnar had been nice enough to not go and watch her in the shower. Thinking back at it, she wished he'd been there. She'd felt alone in there, by herself without him. If anyone was to watch her shower, it was him. But now he was there, and she was still naked and he could ogle her and that made her feel better. Sister Sara arrived a moment later, followed by Sister Fransesca, and they had the boys line up, and explained to them what was about to happen, to the boy's great amusement.

So it was that Alma and her friends spent two whole hours with Sister Sara, teaching the boys to touch and lick pussy, by doing. To her great embarrassment, all the other girls had lined up around them to watch. Sure, they were all naked, but they weren't the ones being fingered, then licked. It was the shower room humiliation all over again.

As she knew, some of the boys already knew their stuff, having gone into the woods with their girlfriends for this purpose often, but she made like she was teaching them something completely new, knowing that the boy's girlfriends were shooting her angry glares as she let them finger her pussy, then lick her. Thta was her way at getting back at them. It was actually nice, when a boy that knew what he was doing gave her a loving nibble and a lick on the clit. She smile at them and gave them a little kiss, and then Sister Fransesca or Sister Maria arrived and cleansed her slit with some rubbing alcohol before the next student arrived to try her out. She didn't get Gunnar, but Liv and Tinna did. She sighed. She was going to have to fuck that man so good to keep him once they got out of this strange place.

A couple of boys were really bad at the pussy examination, seeming not to want to even touch a girl's slit. But they reluctantly did, finishing their course satisfactorily. A few were just clumsy, especially with their fingers, and Alma got her slit plowed painfully by at least three of them, and had to endure that punishment for until she managed to teach them, with the help of Diana. The boys seemed to like fondling Diana, and she liked them fondling her. Her roast-beef looked odd, but it compelled the boys, touching it hypnotized them, and they didn't want to let go. That's how Diana became the last girl to leave, as the boys kept wanting to rub her labia between their fingers, or lick her. She had three boys at one time, one licking her from the front while another one reached past him under her from the front, while another one reached in from behind, meanwhile she rolled her eyes openmouthed in sexual pleasure.

The nuns had to break it up, and they all went their seperate way, not into the woods, now thoroughly guarded by the ever-patrolling nuns.

Alma and Tinna went to bed in each others arms, for comfort. They felt weird after the day, like they had been violated, but at the same time oddly turned on by it. They needed each other's soft physical touch to remedy the strange conflicting feeling. They could run their fingers through each other's slit without plowing, but it still felt better somehow, in their minds, when the boys did it. They finished each other off, softly kissing, and fell asleep.

When they woke up in the morning, still cuddling in each other's arms, they kissed, Frencing each other deeply, and writhed sensuously against each other, their bodies undulating erotically, belly to belly as they warmed up before getting out of bed. Not that any of that was homoerotic in any sort of a lesbian way or anything. Sometimes girls just need to rub their naked bodies against each other and mutually masturbate each other, there's nothing wrong or sexual about that.

19

The boys inspect
the nude girl's vaginas

In the morning the boys stood attention by each wall of the hallway to the shower room as the girls arrived, walking elegantly and unhurriedly past them in the nude, slits uncovered, breasts swinging freely as they took deliberate, sensuous steps past them, asses jiggling with every swaying step; they were giggling and smiling at the boys, who looked so ridiculous in their skirts and knee socks. So unmanly, so humiliated, so erect.

Alma was overjoyed at seeing Gunnar in the line, and she smiled at him and waved, blushing bright red at her own embarrassment. She was, as were all the other girls, beyond covering her private parts, and just proudly swung her arms by her sides as she walked. She could feel the heat of dozens of eyes upon her slit, she could feel the male gaze heat up her ass and it made her breasts tingle and the tingle of embarrassment that she felt all over her body gathered in her slida and turned into moisture as she walked naked past all the staring boys.

The girls had all collectively decided to enjoy showing off their bare asses to the boys, and so they smiled and giggled while waiting for the shower, and took every opportunity to sway their ass and bounce their breasts and make sure the boys all got a good look at their slit, which a few of them had decided to shave clean, so they were perfectly slick and smooth in their thigh gap, all outies in full view. The girls took to standing in front of the boys with their backs straight and shoulders held back and arms behind their back and then slowly gyrate from one side to the other, showing off their whole bodies while asking them some innocent question or other. And the boys watched them, red faced, drooling with desire, their penises hard under the fabric of their tight fitting girl's panties, throbbing and pulsating.

All sense of modesty gone now, none of the girls had the slightest qualm about washing their vagina in front of anyone, and actally rather enjoyed the experience, all under the watchful eye of one of the nuns, who stood by passively. Alma smiled at Gunnar as he stood by the shower door and handed the girls a towel, and waited while they used it until he got it back. He looked ever so uncomfortable, but his friend beside him looked like he enjoyed nothing as much. The girls looked him in the eye as they dried themselves. Alma was a little bit jealous at them, as they squiggled and writhed in front of him, her boyfriend, all naked and wriggling their breasts and exposing their slit to him as they dried their back. Alma didn't remember them needing to dry their back so much before the boys were in charge of the towels. Finally it was Alma's turn, and Gunnar handed her the moist towel, and she looked him in the eye as she calmly dried off most of the water from her body. He looked so awful silly with his make-up.

"I can show you how to apply makeup," she told him, handing him the towel.

"Thanks, but I don't want to aquire that skill."

They smiled at each other.

The girls lined up in their orderly and neat three rows, and smiled as they assumed their position; back straight, feet parted slightly, with their hands on top of their head. Now they weren't about to be fondled by some old, perverted nun, but boys their age, and that excited them, even though the boys were dressed up rather silly, in those girly costumes, the sight of which which made the girls giggle. The atmosphere was very calm and easy now, as the boys paired up, one with a towel and one without, and went to the girls, but only ten of them at this time, and they ran their hands down the girls whole sides, carefully cupping their breasts. Some squeezed them gently. Alma had her breasts squeezed by a boy who made a faint, apologetic smile at her as he did. She smiled at him. He actually kissed her as he slid is fingers through her slit. She kissed him back, that was so nice. He licked his finger and smiled at her, then moved to the next girl, leaving Alma turned on, wanting more.

Each boy did three girls, then changed positions with the towel boy, and the towel boy did three more. Then the next ten boys came, and inspected the girls again in the same way, and then the last five boys came, and did the same, but each of them got to test six girls. They all were red as tomatoes when they finished, and the rumor among the girls was that they had all come while sliding their fingers through the pussy of the sixth girl they tested. Alma found herself being tested five time, but never by Gunnar. But she knew he was there, behind her, testing some other girls.

The final, most important test was now left, the new test, deviced by Sister Sara, and she came in just as the boys were getting in position to administer it to the girls. The boys lined up in front of the girls, and got to their knees. Alma got the boy with the tiny penis. He looked very cute in his schoolgirl dress. She took a deep breath as he held on to her thighs with each hand, and got his face deep there in between and reaching out with his tongue, gently licked her wet slit. She was thoroughly wet after the first set of testing, and that cute little boy got to taste the full strength of her feminine essence. She looked down at him, and he looked up at her, and she saw her pussy fluid leak down his chin, and she smiled. She could already hear moans, as the most sensitive girls orgasmd. She envied them.

Since there were 7 more girls than boys, some of the girls had to wait a little for their turn, and some of the boys got to lick a few more pussies. Alma wondered if Gunnar was one of them, as she stood there in the first line. She wondered if she'd taste all of them individually on his saliva when she kissed him next time. The thought turned her on, and her feminine fluid started dripping down her thigh.

The next boy to lick Alma turned out to be Flemming, and she said "hi" as he looked up to her, having assumed position, and he said "hi" to her. Moans of orgasm were beginning to fill the air as more and more girls got satisfied. Fleming was better at licking pussy than the small dick boy. That was kind of sad, and she decided that she and the other girls must get together and teach him properly how to lick pussy. She was thinking that when Fleming's tongue entered her slida and twirled against her G-spot, and she went all cross-eyed as she let out a soft moan. Her knees went weak and it was hard to stand as the streams of electric pleasure ran out from her vibrating slida through her whole body. Flemming had finished her, and there was one more boy to go.

The third boy just licked her outer labia like some dog would lick a bowl he just emptied. But that was okay, Fleming has brought her to orgasm already. Then he stood up and they smiled at each other before he backed away. She turned around, and saw back over the crowd as the last seven girls were getting theirs.

All the girls were in an easy and a calm and satisfied mood when they all filed out of the shower room. The boys looked hungry and on edge though, and wanting more. Sister Sara followed them, with a mischievous grin.

20

Every day after

The girls loved their new situation. Every day began with the boys being forced to please them orally, and they got a sadistic satisfaction in seeing them squirm with their erections held tight in those tight girl's panties while they got to be naked, feeling the cool breeze flow through their thigs, over their breasts, their belly, their ass. Every day they felt so fresh, so satisfied. And all the boys, with their yearning looks, permanently erect penises, funny walks, drooling mouths, they made them feel beautiful, and not just in comparison. The girls loved to taunt them, swaying their hips when they knew they were looking, standing in front of them, and innocently displaying themselves, asking them questions with sexual implications. About half of them ejaculated before noon, and the classes after that smelled faintly of semen, causing the nuns to make faces.

Every day, the parade of pussy went on, and every day the girls liked it more.

In the evening, they all went to the beach, the boys following the girls. Once there, there the boys finally stripped off their girl's uniforms, releasing their erections, and the girls embraced them, receiving their erections in their slida as nature intended. And they all fucked. They changed partners and fucked again, except Alma and a few other established couples. It was unimaginative but enthusiastic. Afterwards the boys got dressed again, and they all went back to their dormitories.

Epilogue

Gunnar's penis lay erect across Alma's thigh. He had his hand reached around her waist, under her ass, and his finger reaching into her slit, slowly fondling her inner labia. She lay there relaxed, letting him touch her. She let him touch her any way he wanted. He was very creative with his touching. She slowly got moist, and he felt it, and slowly rolled on top of her, his member sliding between her thighs. He reached in between them and took hold of his dick and guided it inside her, and started to slowly fuck her. They had been fucking normally for a while now. No 69, no threesome, no taking it up the ass, just normal him on top, she below, and a slow and steady in and out. They looked each other in the eye as they enjoyed the moment. He was rock hard and filled her moist and slippery slida well as he pumped her, slowly building pace. He made long motions, pulling his member almost all the way out before thrusting back in, and his dick was so long that its tip hit her cervix without his balls touching her at all. She wondered briefly, as she passively lay under him, how it would feel to fuck a man with such a short dick as to have his balls bang against her during sex. She felt her orgasm coming on, and held back a moan. She used to moan, she used to moan loud. He noticed, and leaned in and kissed her, their tongues playing together as he applied lower-back pelvic thrusts to penetrate her. She scratched his back, feeling her pussy empty, then fill, then empty again as he dragged out, and fill again as he stuffed himself into her. She began vibrating, and he could feel it on his penis, the spasms of orgasm, and he came, squirting his load into her, but kept thrusting for a few moments anyway.

She felt as he relaxed, and lay his full weight on top of her, crushing her. She relaxed, enjoying his warm weight on top of her. He didn't pull out of her. He never did. He seemed to enjoy having his member parked inside her slida. He nibbled her ear, and she let him have his peen parked inside her for five more minutes, before rolling him off. She was satisfied. They had pulled it off silently again. They had to do that, so as not to wake up the kids.

The End

www.ingramcontent.com/pod-product-compliance
Lightning Source LLC
Chambersburg PA
CBHW061522120726
48001CB00004B/1388